Contents

KU-485-859

1 Monday

'Oh Lord our Governor, through whose good providence this school has been planted, make it as a field that the Lord has blessed.' Miss Beacon, her tightly permed grey hair haloed by the morning sun which shone through the circular window at the back of the stage, closed her eyes as she prayed for the staff and girls of Critchlowe School.

'Bless our founders and our benefactors; bless all those who work for us and all who love us. Continue the work, oh Lord, which Thou hast wrought in us....' Her voice rang effortlessly through the hall, penetrating to the remotest corner of the garden of daisy-white blouses. 'Preserve in us an unblemished name....'

Bobbie Rippon, kneeling on the non-slip polished parquet floor with the others of 4N, gazed up at the Headmistress, half-hypnotised by the dazzling disc of light behind Miss Beacon's head. The early October sun had climbed no more than level with the building and Bobbie saw the brilliant window with out-of-focus intensity, vermilion tinged and blurred at the edges like a fireball.

Fire. They would never get out. People screaming, climbing over each other, feet in hard-heeled shoes treading into faces, splitting the flesh from a cheekbone, slicing away a nose or a lip....

'Nourish in us the spirit of a wholesome discipline....'

Fanny Anthony nudged Bobbie with her elbow and whispered, 'Balls!' Bobbie gasped with the shock of her sudden return to reality, then smothered a giggle of amusement at Fanny's profanity. It was a relief to be released from the bad dream.

'Amen. Our Father. . . .'

'Which art in Heaven . . .' Bobbie joined in thankfully. It was all right as long as there was something to do, because then the nightmares did not sneak up and try to take advantage of her inattention. And with proper care, nothing dreadful would happen. Good would prevail.

'For thine is the Kingdom, the Power and the Glory, for ever and ever, Amen.'

With a noisy, relieved upheaval, the school rearranged itself more comfortably.

'Pagan bloody ritual,' muttered Fanny, rubbing her knees as she sat cross-legged beside Bobbie. 'It's a wonder they don't have human sacrifices.'

Mrs Newley, their form mistress, perceiving rather than hearing Fanny's irreverence, raised shocked eyebrows. Fanny raised her own in reply, but with an expression of clear-eyed innocence.

The Head Girl stood up to read the notices and was in turn silhouetted in front of the window. Bobbie stared down into the dark comfort of her navy-blue skirt. She would not be caught again. Not for a while, anyway. In a minute they would go back to form rooms to collect their books, and then to geography and then to English and at twenty to eleven it would be break time, cold outside in the yard but safe from imaginings. School was all right really, most of the time.

The girls of 4N stood, approximately in line, outside the door of Miss Perkins' room, lethargically glad to be back in the warm building after break. One or two carried satchels or briefcases but most of them simply clutched their books in armfuls. Rosie Mowlem had an absurdly bulging music case while Sandie McIver clasped an inadequate paper carrier in both arms. Bobbie Rippon, whose hair stuck out round her head like a frizzy dandelion clock, dangled a straw basket with unravelling handles and Fanny Anthony leaned against the wall with her hands in her pockets, all her books in a cardboard box at her feet.

Bobbie stared into the middle distance, observing the resulting blurry shapes of colour around her with interest. It was a half-involuntary technique which she had developed at an early age, a private retreat where shouting faces were reduced to red blobs and boring surroundings became a misty dreamland. She was aware of the snares which her escapist habit presented and vowed again and again, like a repentant nail biter, that she would overcome it and yet, in the same way that she did in fact bite her nails, Bobbie could not break free of her daydreams.

At the moment she gazed happily at the curious pattern of white blouses around her, reflecting that they looked rather like snow-clad mountains, riven by striped ties as though avalanches had carved gulleys through them.

Miss Perkins arrived, fitted her key into the door and turned briskly to face the girls. This form always managed to look particularly slovenly, she thought, and peculiarly non-uniform. They had aggressive, immodestly feminine hips and busts. Several of them could do with a good firm roll-on but then, girls didn't bother about such things these days. Regrettably, most of them managed to make their school uniform look like ordinary clothes. There was a time when grammar school children looked reasonably impersonal and communication took place on a purely academic level. These girls threatened to approach far too closely, Miss Perkins decided. That's why young teachers like Miss Ross were having trouble. The structure of respect which held everyone slightly apart was breaking down.

Miss Perkins pursed her lips and stared concentratedly at the straggly line of slouching, hip-jutting girls until they shuffled themselves into some semblance of order. There was no need to waste words on so routine a matter. She opened the door and entered her room, followed by the girls of 4N.

Fanny Anthony pushed her cardboard box, which was stamped 'Gordon's Gin, 12 Bottles', along the floor with one foot, instead of picking it up and carrying it. Miss Perkins took this to be a gesture of contempt.

'Fanny! Have you nothing more suitable to bring your

9

books to school in than a cardboard box?'

'No, Miss Perkins.'

'The school rules require you to provide yourself with a briefcase or satchel.'

'Yes, Miss Perkins.'

Fanny's face was devoid of expression but her voice betrayed a fatal trace of resignation. Miss Perkins, like all experienced teachers, possessed mental antennae acutely sensitive to such nuances. Certain that Fanny's parents were reasonably well off, she struck back hard.

'If you are telling me, Fanny, that your father is too poverty-stricken to be able to buy you some kind of cheap case, then I advise you to notify Miss Beacon of that fact. There are funds available to help genuine welfare cases.'

Fanny glared at her furiously but said nothing. Miss Perkins sat down, dismissively.

Fanny, in the relatively safe harbour of a desk near the back of the room, got out her maths books and the typescript of the play which the Theatre Centre were performing at half term. She had, for the first time, got a decent part and she was determined to be word-perfect by the weekend.

'Simultaneous quadratics,' announced Miss Perkins. 'You should all know these by now but I'll go through it once more for the sake of anyone whose memory is a little less than perfect.'

Only maths teachers, Bobbie Rippon thought, could write numbers in the kind of fluent way that looked like handwriting. She glanced round at Fanny and saw her head bowed over her desk. Gosh! She wasn't upset about what Miss Perkins had said, was she? People shouldn't say awful things like that about welfare. Suppose there was a desperately poor girl in the class, trying to keep up appearances. Bobbie, why do you bring your books to school in a box? The handle came off my briefcase, Miss, because it's so old. Why doesn't your mother buy you a new one? My mother's dead, Miss.

Bobbie gave a little gasp of horror. Thoughts that crept up unnoticed like that might actually happen. She must nail it down and ask for it not to happen, then it wouldn't. Cross fingers, touch wood, no black dress, no lilies in the front room, no being sent away to a Children's Home and wearing second-hand clothes. Please, God.

'Roberta Rippon, get on with your work.'

Exercise 23, page 47, numbers 1–12. Bobbie turned over the pages busily, glad to be safe again.

Miss Perkins patrolled slowly up the left-hand aisle and back, surveying the exercise books. Up the centre aisle and back; up the right-hand aisle—

'Fanny Anthony, what are you doing?'

Fanny did not move. The position of her hands, disappearing under the centre-parted curtain of straight brown hair, suggested that she had her fingers in her ears. The rest of the girls in the class watched delightedly. There was about to be a drama.

Miss Perkins tapped the girl on the shoulder, instinct assuring her that it was not simultaneous quadratic equations which engrossed Fanny so deeply. Fanny jerked her head upright and muttered an apology, trying as she did so to slide her reading matter underneath her text book. Miss Perkins held out an imperious hand.

'Oh, no, please, Miss Perkins, I won't look at it again but I honestly do need to keep it,' said Fanny. 'It's my part.'

Miss Perkins' outstretched hand did not waver.

'Oh, all *right*.' Fanny sat back to allow a clear view of her desk. Miss Perkins picked up the sheaf of duplicated papers and turned it back to the title page.

'*Us – Lot*', she read, pronouncing the two words with slow distaste. She gave a faint smile. 'I am surprised, Fanny, that you should find this kind of ungrammatical rubbish so fascinating. Who is the author – Shakespeare? Shaw?' She lifted her glasses a little with one hand, extending the script to peer at it more effectively. The girls giggled. 'Ibsen? Ah, here we are – "K. Olliphant". Is that a famous name?' She gazed round at the girls. 'Should I have *heard* of Kathleen Olliphant? Or is it Keith Olliphant? Have I missed out, as they say, on some new and momentous development in English literature?'

Fanny had turned very red. 'It's Ken, actually,' she muttered. The girls, always ready to react to the mention of a male name, screamed with laughter. Miss Perkins waited for it to subside, then said, 'Yes. Well, Fanny, since you are clearly God's gift to the contemporary theatre, perhaps you would like to demonstrate your talent in other directions. Come along.'

She walked briskly back to her desk, where she deposited Fanny's play script. Then she rubbed the blackboard clean of the demonstration equation, leaving only the first line which stated the problem. She handed the chalk to Fanny.

'The stage, Miss Bernhardt, is yours.'

In that moment, Fanny hated Miss Perkins very bitterly. She knew the formula for simultaneous quadratics perfectly well. There was no need to go on learning the same thing over and over again. Neither was there any need for this stupid fuss. She'd *said* she was sorry. Fanny began to work the equation on the blackboard, noticing irritably that her figures looked clumsy and amateurish below Miss Perkins' neat, assured ones. Why did teachers have to behave like animal trainers, she raged inwardly.

Fanny's anger destroyed her concentration. She heard a quick collective intake of breath from the class and realised that she had made an error. She stared at the figures, trying to see the slip but listening at the same time for whispered advice. None came, and in the effort of listening for it, the figures were suddenly meaningless.

Miss Perkins watched with satisfaction. She allowed Fanny's confusion to continue just long enough to appear ludicrous, but she did not make the mistake of allowing her to recover. With a leisurely, despairing gesture, she wiped the blackboard clean, dusting her hands afterwards with a gloomy resignation calculated to make the girls laugh. Girls, she had decided long ago, were essentially treacherous and could always be relied on to join the winning side. It was deeply ingrained in them to behave thus, or so Miss Perkins believed, because of the survival technique of the primitive female. She had to mate, willy-nilly, with whichever male won the fight for her favours or survived the multiple hazards of jungle life. In depressed or lonely moments, Miss Perkins had derived great comfort from the thought that women are capable of intellectual honesty only when they are free from the impulse to behave as their sexual responses demand. She smiled at 4N, waiting for them to settle down.

At that moment, both Fanny and Miss Perkins felt a contempt for the giggling, malicious crowd but, where Miss Perkins savoured a familiar pleasure in the situation, Fanny was overwhelmed by furious, miserable resentment. She was experiencing, not for the first time, a sense of betrayal – but this time she was beginning to suspect that the behaviour of her form mates was not merely unsurprising but normal.

Bobbie, with great courage, caught Fanny's eye and gave her a quick smile of support, Sandie McIver looked out of the window in a distant sort of way and Rosie Mowlem dropped a pencil. They were changing sides again.

'Well, Fanny,' said Miss Perkins at once, but with apparent kindness, 'you *did* come unstuck, didn't you? Shall we go through it together?'

'I know where I went wrong,' said Fanny, whose brain had cleared. 'If you hadn't rubbed it off I'd have done it.' But Miss Perkins was ahead of her, chalking in the neat pattern of figures with contemptuous ease. 'Perhaps,' she said as she worked, 'you would care to rejoin the audience?'

The girls giggled again but as Fanny sat down there were glances of sympathy. In ten minutes they would escape from the classroom and then, in the neutrality of the corridor, their loyalties would all be to each other.

Miss Perkins glanced at her watch. Ten minutes of good, hard work now. What a pity poor Miss Ross could not have witnessed that little scene. It was the kind of thing which could teach a new member of staff so much.

The late afternoon light was already fading as the girls

streamed out of school, down its tarmac paths between the hard-pruned roses and out through the four minor gates. The imposing wrought-iron ones which led to the front door were out of bounds to pupils.

The wind blew wet and cold across the flat landscape and the bare lime trees shed fragments of twig into the muddy road. Not for the first time, Bobbie conjured up an imaginary tidal wave, a Hokusai-high wall of water thrust along the Thames by a freak wind from the North Sea, spilling over the low-lying land and sweeping away the football posts and the home-going girls in a watery mass of branches and hats, plaits and hands and satchels, screaming, drowning ... could she climb a tree?

Bobbie stared at the nearest lime tree, its black trunk devoid of branches for fully five metres. She could not climb that. But, confronted with the tree's reality, the nightmare faded. Bobbie stepped sideways to avoid a puddle. Critchlowe girls were not allowed to wear wellingtons, despite the muddy condition of the roads. Wellingtons, in Miss Beacon's eyes, were a self-indulgence; a passport to sloppy behaviour and untold permissiveness. A little asceticism, a trace of self-denial was, in her view, the corner-stone of virtue.

'Hi! Bobbie – wait for me!'

Fanny Anthony came running after Bobbie, coat unbuttoned and long hair flying, her cardboard box of books clutched in both arms. She caught up, panting.

'Went to try and get my script back.'

'No luck?'

'She'd gone, mingy old bitch. Saw that new one.'

'Miss Ross.'

'Yes. She seems almost human.'

Bobbie grinned. Fanny had decided ideas about the staff, as about everything. 'Miss Perkins always goes early,' she said. 'On her bicycle.'

'But *why*?' demanded Fanny furiously. 'She hasn't got any kids or anything – she can't be an unmarried mum at her age. And she sure is unmarried.'

Bobbie giggled, her frizzy hair blown even wilder by the wind. She was frequently shocked by Fanny's violence of opinion and of expression but she never failed to be amused by her. Fanny exaggerated everything and made tremendous fusses which were often silly, but she was never dull. There was never time to think too much when Fanny was about.

'*Well*,' Fanny added impatiently, 'what a cowy thing to do. She *knew* I wanted it back. It just shows how much she hates school, the way she belts off home. She doesn't give a damn about us. Fancy being taught by a woman like that. She's not *normal*.'

'Lots of people aren't normal,' said Bobbie. 'Perhaps you're not. Or I'm not.'

'That's just being smug. No, I think teachers ought to be real people, not just calculating machines. They ought to be taken away from teaching occasionally and made to do other jobs. They ought to be forced into contact with other people. They ought to have families – or at least they ought to have friends and lovers and things. But I mean, can you imagine old Perkins with a man? She wouldn't know what to do with him. He'd fetch up with "Good work" written on his thing in red ink.'

Bobbie gave a shriek of scandalised laughter. 'Or "Must try harder"!' she added. This amused them both so much that they leaned on each other for support.

Iris Newley, 4N's form mistress, was driving homewards in her elderly car when she drew level with the two staggering figures. She pulled to a halt and wound down the window.

'I *thought* it was you two,' she said. 'God, what a mess! Roberta, where's your hat? And yours, Fanny?'

'Mine doesn't go on, really,' said Bobbie, looking worried. 'It's my hair, you see. It's so frizzy. It pushes it off all the time.'

Iris Newley snorted. 'And what feeble excuse have *you* got, Fanny?'

'None,' said Fanny baldly.

'Have you *got* a hat?'

'Oh, yes, it's about somewhere.'

'Then, damn it, girl, *wear* the bloody thing. I want to see you both tomorrow morning. With hats. Got it?'

'Got it,' said Fanny.

'Yes, Mrs Newley,' added Bobbie quickly, seeing an ominous flush of colour sweep over the teacher's face. 'We will, honestly.'

Iris Newley fought down an urgent desire to get out of the car and slap Fanny Anthony's face. That cool-eyed, insolent little bitch was a thoroughly bad influence on Roberta Rippon, no doubt about it.

'All right,' she said, controlling her rage, 'tomorrow. And don't forget.'

She let the clutch in and accelerated away as fast as her eight-year-old Morris Minor would go. The rear wheels spattered the girls with gravel.

'Oh, charming!' said Fanny, glaring after the car. 'Now, her I *can't* stand. All those damns and bloodies, trying to show how open-minded she is, when really she's just as petty as the rest of them. I don't know why you don't stand up to her, Bob. You are a *coward*.'

'I think it's silly, going around sticking your neck out,' said Bobbie. 'You'll only get reported to Miss Beacon or something. You might just as well *pretend* to be cooperative, even if you know in your own mind that you don't believe it. If you keep your thoughts private, people can't get at them.'

'That's hypocrisy,' said Fanny. 'Why *should* I pretend? Look' – she settled to one of her favourite themes – 'if people can't be honest with each other then you can't have any real relationships between them, can you?'

Bobbie frowned. 'But – well – you just *can't* say exactly what you think, can you? Not always.'

'I can,' said Fanny obstinately. 'In any case, who's interested in what we think? The sort of work they want at school is just mindless repetition. Remember what you're told and trot it all out again when asked. The ideal pupil would be a walking tape recorder.'

16

'Oh, *Fanny*!'

'Well, it would! They don't want you to *think*! That's the trouble with her.' Fanny nodded in the direction taken by Iris Newley's car. 'She wants to seem all modern but what happens in those so-called "discussion" lessons she takes? The minute anyone mentions democracy in action or legalising pot, she takes fright and changes the subject. She *hates* you thinking. I'd rather have old Ma Perkins than Mrs Newley. She may be out of the Ark but at least she's consistent in her own ghastly way.'

Bobbie was suddenly smitten by an idea and, for once, she did not stop to consider it before she spoke. 'The trouble with you, Fanny, is you've got such a nice home. Everything else seems awful by comparison, and it's not *that* awful. I mean, that new teacher, Miss Ross – I think she's quite nice.'

'M'm. Maybe.' But Fanny lacked conviction.

Iris Newley stopped her car in the drive and got out to unlock the garage doors. Wild yapping sounded from inside the house. 'All right, sweetie!' she called. 'Mummy's coming!'

Having put the car away, she let herself into the house and was at once aware of an unpleasant smell. When she opened the kitchen door the thick, sour reek was overwhelming, and she saw at once that the green marble-effect vinyl floor was smeared and puddled with copious quantities of excrement. 'Oh, *Monty*!' she said. 'Not again! What ever's the matter with you?'

The very obese Jack Russell terrier crept to her feet, eye whites showing. Diving quickly, he turned on his back, his distended pink stomach defencelessly upwards. His head was held slightly sideways so that he could continue to gaze up with one bulging brown eye at his mistress who, seen in her thus upside-down position, seemed much less likely to hit him with a newspaper.

Mary Ross was tired and depressed. It was a long walk up the hill from Critchlowe School to her digs and besides, the day's teaching had, as usual, been exhausting. She reached the large Victorian house in which she had recently taken a furnished room and climbed the stone steps which led up to the front door. Dumping her briefcase, she fished in her handbag for her key.

In more cheerful moments, Mary had found the overblown ornamentation of the front door amusing; tonight its pomposity merely annoyed her. Had the house ever been so important as to deserve all that intricate moulding and sand-blasted glass? If so, it must now feel ashamed of the many crudely screwed-on bell pushes which adorned the cracked paint covering its mahogany door jamb.

Mary picked up her pint of milk from the doorstep and let herself in. The hall was sombre and smelt faintly damp. Very little light penetrated the grimy ornate windows and the wall-paper was dark brown, patterned with autumn leaves. She started up the stairs, gazing determinedly at the brown lino so as to avoid looking at Mrs Mallalieu's picture. Mrs Mallalieu, Mary's landlady, went to art classes and her most triumphant achievement was a portrait of a middle-aged woman which, Mary felt uneasily, probably represented the artist herself. It hung in the middle of an oval patch of paler wallpaper where a mirror had been taken down to accommodate it.

Despite her resolution, Mary's eyes strayed to the picture. The salmon-pink paint was streaky and toffee-like and the artist had suffered from a narrowness of vision which had resulted in a series of localised struggles. The left eye had given trouble, and so had the dark grey shadow under the chin. The mouth had been scraped out and repainted several times and the nose was a Flodden Field of dead colour. Two slightly lop-sided jet black nostrils glared out from the centre of the face, challenged for pride of place by a smeary titanium white highlight in the left eye. In between lay an area of brown paint which reminded Mary of a disused quarry she and her brother used to play in as children.

Irritated, she found that she had actually paused on the stairs to look at the beastly thing. She went on up, burdened with her briefcase, handbag and pint of milk, turned and walked along the landing, then climbed the second flight of stairs which had straight, thin banisters made of varnished deal instead of the bulbous mahogany ones on the lower flight.

Poor Victorians! thought Mary. How it would grieve them to know that the standards which had survived were those of the servants rather than of the masters! No cut glass and mahogany in modern houses – just plain deal. She let herself into her room, stood the milk on the table, kicked the door shut behind her and flopped down on to the pink candlewick-covered bed, which smelt slightly of soap. In that first moment of relaxation, her eyes flooded with hot, easy tears. She blinked them away, rubbed them with an impatient hand. She was breathing in short outward sighs, her lungs refilling with lazy shallowness as though she was already deeply asleep. It was impossible to forget the events of the day.

Perhaps, Mary thought, she ought not to have taken a job in an all-girls' school. It had seemed much easier to keep order at the mixed school where she had done her teaching practice, even though she had once lifted a boy to his feet by a handful of his hair. That incident had given her nightmares for weeks about angry parents and court cases for assault but, as the senior master had soothingly pointed out, she *had* asked the boy twice already to stand up. Furthermore, since he was a third of a metre taller than she was, it seemed unlikely that he would want the incident publicised.

But 4N were a different thing altogether. There was a cool deliberation about their misbehaviour which made it perfectly clear that Mary was being put on trial and so far, Mary had completely failed. Three weeks of the term had gone and they still did not accept her as a teacher, let alone respect her. Today they had hummed. It was a tuneless, absent-minded hum, each girl appearing to be engrossed in her work, but whenever Mary spoke, the humming rose to a chorus of wordless derision which almost drowned her voice. 'Do *stop* it!' she had shouted at last. 'It's just beastly rude of you – and so *silly* – you're more intelligent than that!' And then Miss Perkins had come in.

Miss Perkins, of course, had quelled them with a single, long stare. She had then apologised to Mary on 4N's behalf for their discourtesy 'to a teacher who is still very new to our school and our ways. Would you,' she asked them, 'treat a visitor to your own home in such a way as to make her feel embarrassed and unwanted?' A few of the girls had looked bored but several had reddened and stared down at their books. After Miss Perkins' departure they had preserved a neutral semblance of good behaviour but at the end of the lesson they had left the room with unnecessarily loud chatter and bursts of derisive laughter.

Mary stared at the ceiling. The light fitting which dangled on a brown flex contained a large bakelite adaptor socket from which a further flex, tacked at one point to the picture rail, led to a bedside light. Another ran to an unoccupied plug which was secured by a piece of sticking plaster to the mirror over the fireplace, clearly rigged up for an electric shaver. She intended to use it for an extra light so that she could use the mirror for applying make-up instead of squinting at herself in a handbag mirror under the central light. And perhaps when next month's salary came, she might get a toaster. Luxury!

Mary sighed. Three years at Bristol University reading English and a year's post-graduate teacher training – and here she was, aching all over and staring at the ceiling in a squalid little room, having taught nobody anything – ever. What's more, she told herself, rubbing salt into her wounds, the way things were going, she never would. The school seemed a depressing place, dominated by its academic syllabus and suspicious of any form of creativity – but Mary was in no mood to off-load the blame on to external circumstances. At the very least, she would take the responsibility for her own failure.

She swung her legs to the floor and sat up. Her feet ached, and she was hungry. A tin of chicken soup, she promised herself, then scrambled eggs, and coffee with the top of the milk in it. But first of all she would have a good, long, hot, relaxing bath. With bubbles.

Opening the door to the bathroom, Mary thought again how much it looked like a cross between a ship's boiler room and the Cheddar Gorge. It was very narrow and had a high ceiling where years of unventilated steam had caused grey leprous growths to sprout through the dark green peeling paint. A profusion of pipes decked the walls with leaden macaroni and, looming over the bath, stood the Sentry Ideal Domestic Water Heater.

Mary had recognised it at first sight as a simple old-fashioned geyser. There was perhaps something cranky about the way it wore its iron Chinese coolie hat but otherwise it seemed orthodox enough. Mounted halfway up the wall, it offered two short metal arms level with the user's chest and a brass plate bore 'Instructions For Use', long illegible with green corrosion. Mary, however, was an experienced geyser user. She put a fivepenny piece into the slot of the comparatively new meter and turned the handle round until the coin fell. She put the plug in the immense greyish bath and moved the geyser's knobby arms across to the 'On' position. She turned on the water tap and, as a trickle of as yet unheated water began to flow from the geyser, went hurriedly back to her room to undress. She preferred not to be in the bathroom with the geyser when it lit its gas. She was safely behind her own door – after a rapid scuttle across the landing – when she heard the geyser light with a ferocious bang.

There were several flakes of plaster floating in the bath water when Mary returned to the bathroom but at least the water was beautifully hot.

'It's nice when you get to the paved bit,' said Bobbie as she and Fanny turned into Wilmot Road. 'You don't have to keep looking out for puddles.'

Fanny sniffed appreciatively at the sweet scent of sawdust which came from the timber yard behind the railway station. 'Back to civilisation,' she agreed. 'You know, I'd like to go to a really *slummy* school with high railings and a chip shop next door and *boys*.'

'Would you really? I don't think I would.'

'Yes, really. Some school that's bang in the middle of great blocks of flats and pubs and betting shops. Somewhere where you can see *people* out of the windows, not just grotty old tennis courts. Our place is like a desert island.'

'You are funny!' said Bobbie – and then she suddenly gripped Fanny's arm. 'Listen!'

From a blank-looking warehouse across the street came the sound of somebody playing a trumpet. The sweet, melancholy notes had the same beguiling appeal as the smell of bacon cooked in the fresh air. Unmistakably, it was no radio or record player which produced the music. This was the real thing.

Following her nose with the eagerness of a gun dog, Bobbie trotted across the road and stood gazing up at the blank windows, which were painted inside with greenish-tinted whitewash. A fascia board running the length of the building above the first floor windows bore a pattern of rain-washed rust marks showing where the name of a manufacturing company had once been nailed up in huge letters. It seemed an unlikely setting in which to find a jazz trumpeter but the music undoubtedly came from behind one of the featureless windows. The trumpeter was playing a blues, the notes lazy and poignant, cynical and yet nostalgic. Suddenly he abandoned his reflective mood and broke into ragtime, hitting the double tempo with sparkling, punchy notes.

'Oh, get that!' shouted Bobbie, alight with excitement. 'Let's dance!' She broke into a wild cakewalk, swinging her basket of books with abandoned delight. Fanny put her box down on the pavement and joined in, not to be outdone. People stared at the two cavorting schoolgirls and Fanny grinned back at them. Bobbie, on the other hand, was unaware of their presence, swept up in a world of pure delight where everyone danced under a hot black sky scented with magnolia blossom.

Suddenly, in mid-phrase, the music stopped. In the bleak silence which succeeded it, voices were heard faintly from the upstairs room. Evidently someone had come in to talk to the trumpeter.

'Perhaps he'll start again in a minute,' Bobbie said hopefully.

'M'm. Don't think I'll wait,' said Fanny. 'The twins'll be home and I'd better make sure they don't gobble up something Helen's left for supper. You know, Bob, you're very good at dancing.'

Bobbie was still gazing up at the window from which the music had come. 'Yes,' she said absently, 'I did ballet for ages when I was little but Mum said I was never going to be really brilliant so she made me stop.'

'But why?'

'I was growing too big. Prima ballerinas are always tiny. The silly thing is, I didn't go on growing for long and I'd have been all right. Do wait for a bit, Fanny – I'm sure he'll play some more in a minute.'

'No. Can't.' Fanny set off resolutely along the road. 'You coming?' she called over her shoulder.

'Oh, all right.' Reluctantly, Bobbie caught up her friend. 'But Fan, who is it? I mean, why in that funny sort of factory place?'

'Oh, it's one of the Brethren. They've got quite a good group, actually. They practise in the evenings and all the old stogies round here keep complaining.'

'What d'you mean, the Brethren? Is that the name of the group?'

'No – haven't you seen them? You must have done, Bob – that Biblical lot with the long hair and sandals. The girls all look as if they're wearing bedspreads. It's a sort of community, peace and love and all that. Share everything.'

'And they live in that funny place?'

'That's right. It used to be a factory and then it was used as some sort of warehouse and now they're in it. Been there for months.'

'But what do they do about money?'

'Haven't the foggiest. They've got an old ambulance painted

with psychedelic flowers – there it is, look, parked across the road. I've seen them unloading rather grotty looking vegetables from it sometimes and I think they go and scrounge the leftovers from shops and things. None of them actually seems to work. They hand out a lot of leaflets about God, though.'

'How super.'

'What – God?'

'No, I mean living all together like that.'

'I'd hate it. I want to get really good at something so I can earn lots of money and have things the way I want them. Or even if I've got no money, I'd rather be on my own. Fancy having to consult other people all the time!'

'I think it sounds lovely,' said Bobbie. 'Like being part of a big family. You'd always *belong*. I mean, school's all right, but it's so easy to get sort of switched off.'

'You can say that again! The trouble with school is, they think you're their property. Potential gold letters on the board in the entrance hall. Stuffed, like the first Mrs Thurber.'

'Who's Mrs Thurber?'

Fanny sighed. 'Really, you are illiterate sometimes. You know the man who wrote *Thurber's Dogs*? James Thurber?'

'Yes.'

'Well, he did a cartoon where he's ushering someone into the room, saying, "... and this is the *first* Mrs Thurber". And there's this woman on all fours on top of the wardrobe. It doesn't *say* she's stuffed but she looks as if she is.'

'Ergh! How horrible. Honestly, Fan, you have got a disgusting sense of humour.'

'Yes,' said Fanny complacently, 'I think I have, really. Very fashionable. Black comedy and all that.' She stopped, put her box down, held out both arms in a crucified position and added, 'What a lousy way to spend Easter.' Then she picked up the box and walked on. Bobbie was shocked. 'No wonder Mrs Newley thinks you're awful.'

Fanny shrugged. 'It's only awful if you believe it – and if you believe it, then it doesn't matter whether other people do or not, does it?'

'I think there are some things you shouldn't joke about. I mean, I'm not *sure*.'

'So you think you'd better not be too cheeky in case a dirty great hand comes out of the sky and knocks you flat? Oh, Bob, don't be so silly. You *can't* believe in the Virgin Birth and the miracles and all that stuff. I mean, it's practically *voodoo*.'

Bobbie hesitated. 'Well, I know there are scientific explanations for lots of things that people thought were acts of God,' she said. 'Evolution and all that. But – well, it doesn't answer everything, does it?'

'Of course it does,' said Fanny. 'It's just a question of accepting that there's a lot we haven't understood yet. That's where the act of faith bit comes in, when you have to admit that we're only tiny atoms in the vast unknown.'

'But I don't *want* to think of it like that. It's so depressing – and sort of frightening, too. I used to love it when I was little and we used to say that prayer at the Infants' School, "Gentle Jesus, meek and mild". He used to seem like a real person, with that lovely soft brown beard.'

'Perhaps you're a mystic,' said Fanny. 'Like Saint Joan. You don't hear voices, do you?'

Bobbie sighed. 'Not when there aren't any,' she said.

They walked on in silence until they came to Fanny's house. It looked like a brick-built country cottage, complete with criss-cross leaded windows and gabled roof, but was much bigger than any genuine cottage would have been. A tarmac-surfaced car park occupied all the ground from the pavement to the front door and at the gate a gilt-lettered board announced, 'Dr Stewart Anthony. Dr Richard Bryant.' Below this was pinned a piece of paper which read, 'Consulting hours have been replaced by an appointments system. Please telephone before 9.30 a.m.'

'Oh!' remarked Bobbie, noticing this. 'Is your dad having a revolution?'

'Sort of. The poor dears were sitting in the waiting room in *droves*, all blowing germs over each other for hours – and talk about grumble!'

'Well, it makes you feel grumbly if you've waited ages. Does it work better, this new system?'

'Stewart thinks so,' said Fanny. 'You coming in?'

Bobbie hesitated. 'Well – just for a minute. Got masses of homework.'

They went past the surgery door and round to the side of the house where the kitchen was.

'Food!' said Fanny, dumping her box on the table and gazing round the kitchen in a predatory way. 'Must have food! Now, what is there?' She snatched open the fridge door. 'Ah, cold chicken!'

'There's a note on the table,' Bobbie pointed out.

'From Helen, I expect,' said Fanny. She picked up the note and read out, 'Darlings – Do *not* eat cold chicken in fridge. It's for pie tonight with tin of mushrooms, etc. Please get out fro. pastry to thaw. Love, H.'

Bobbie laughed. 'I thought you said it was the boys who ate the wrong things!' she said. 'Where do you get out fro. pastry from?'

'The free., of course,' said Fanny, delving into the deep freeze. 'Here we are – I'll stick it on top of the boiler, it'll be fine in half an hour. Must eat something, I'm *ravenous*, aren't you? What about a bacon sandwich?'

'That would be super – but are you sure your mum won't mind?'

'No, she'd have said in the note if there was an embargo on bacon. That's the great thing about working mothers, they don't fuss about details. They can't, poor dears. Too frantic, running about Doing Their Thing.'

'I wish *my* mother worked,' said Bobbie. 'The only thing she does is the house. Or nothing at all. That's worse, really.'

Fanny put four rashers of bacon on the grill pan. 'It's super, though, your house,' she said. 'All those fitted carpets and things. I mean, you never have knobs missing off cupboards and cardboard boxes full of things like scooter wheels and perished football innards. But then, you don't have brothers. They're the ones who muck things up.'

'No, we don't!' shouted Matthew, bouncing into the kitchen. 'I just *heard* that, you rotten old snide!'

'Good,' retorted Fanny, 'then perhaps you'll clear up a bit. Where's Dominic?'

'Making something in the sitting room. He says it's a new kind of hydrofoil. Are you cooking bacon?'

'Yes. D'you want some?'

'Please! Dominic had some cold baked beans and pickled onions and it quite put me off eating anything else. I don't know why he eats such ghastly things.'

'Get another rasher out of the fridge, then.'

'*Two* rashers,' said Matthew.

Colin McIver coughed politely. 'Half past five, Mrs Anthony,' he said.

Helen Anthony looked at him across the head of her browsing customer with a slight frown. 'If you are in a hurry, Colin,' she said primly, 'do go, of course.'

'Oh, I'm so sorry,' said the customer, coming upright, 'am I keeping you?'

'Not a bit,' said Helen.

'Well, I think I'll take this, anyway. I always feel I'm safe with Enid Blyton.'

'I'm sure you are,' said Helen. 'That'll be thirty-five pence, please.'

The woman sighed as she scrabbled for money in her purse. 'I don't know, these children with their books and whatnot, they do cost an awful lot of money, don't they?'

'Do you think that books are really expensive?' asked Colin in his serious Scottish voice. 'That's very interesting – you see, I feel that books are relatively cheap in this country by comparison with other European nations.'

'Let me give you a bag,' said Helen.

'And, of course, compared with other consumer goods,' said Colin.

'Thank you very much. I do hope I haven't made you late.'
The customer gathered up her handbag, shopping bag and
book and made for the door, glancing uneasily at Colin.
'Goodbye!'

Colin opened the door for her. 'Bye-bye,' he said gravely –
then closed the door and turned the Open sign to Closed.

'Colin, you are naughty.'

'Why?'

'You shouldn't make speeches about the economics of book-
selling to my poor little Blyton-buying customers. It makes
them feel embarrassed.'

'So they jolly well should be. They come in here, to a
specialist children's bookshop, and then try to make you feel
guilty about taking their miserable thirty-five pence. What does
she think you are?'

'But I expect it's a lot of money to her.'

'So what? If she intended to buy, then she must have
reckoned on spending at least that much. After all, she doesn't
have to buy anything, so why is she grumbling? It's not as if
you're charging your own price for something you grow in
your back garden – *you're* not the publisher.'

Helen laughed, shaking her head. 'You're an intolerant lot,
you young things,' she said.

'We're not!' protested Colin. 'I listen very patiently to
people's daft ideas about what their children should read!'

'There you go again. "Daft ideas" you say. These people,
as you call them, know their children better than you do. At
the age of eighteen I shouldn't think you know children at all.'

'Nineteen, if you don't mind, Mrs Anthony,' said Colin
with dignity. 'And I would point out that I have two younger
sisters and a three-year-old baby brother. And I'd rather be
thought intolerant than hypocritical.'

Helen turned slightly pink. 'Colin! Are you accusing *me* of
being hypocritical? I don't always say exactly what I think to
customers, I admit – but it's not just a question of making a
sale. It's the whole business of being kind to people. Politeness,
if you like. Social oil.'

Colin grinned. 'Don't mind me. It's just my Scottish up-bringing. If you go into a bookshop in Dundee and ask an assistant what he thinks, he'll tell you what he thinks. And that doesn't mean what he thinks you *want* him to think.'

'M'm. Well, I didn't have a Scottish upbringing and I still regard it as thoroughly unkind to make people doubt their own judgement. It's a sort of mental bullying. And anyway,' Helen added, 'you can't count that sister of yours as a child any more. Sandie's in Fanny's class at school and those great lumping girls aren't children!'

'They read children's books,' objected Colin. 'Sandie was reading *Peter Pan* the other day, would you believe it? She said the Darlings were absolute monsters. The worst parents in the world. Specially Mr Darling. She thought he was a raving psychopath.'

'I'm going home,' announced Helen. 'I can see that I'm getting absolutely nowhere in this argument, so I may as well do my housewife and mother bit. Do you want a lift?'

'No thanks,' said Colin. 'I'm going to do my fresh air and exercise bit.'

'Fanny! It's twenty to six!' Bobbie jumped to her feet, scat-tering pieces of paper and copies of *Jackie* over Fanny's bed-room floor.

'So what?' said Fanny, who had changed into jeans and lay sprawled comfortably across her bed.

'Well, Mum gets into a tizz if I'm late. She says she imagines me lying in the road, being covered with a red blanket. And the police ringing up and saying, "Mrs Rippon, I'm afraid I have some bad news for you." '

'She wouldn't worry so much if she was busier,' said Fanny. 'She wouldn't have time. Doesn't she do *anything*?'

'Oh, coffee mornings,' said Bobbie. 'And bridge, of course. She's mad about bridge. I think she's quite good at it.'

'I can't imagine liking cards,' said Fanny. 'Sitting round a little table, calculating away like mad to see if you can arrange the numbers in a certain way – so *trivial!*'

'I don't know.' Bobbie was cautious. 'I've played a bit, and it's fascinating in a way, once you get going. Get *going*!' she repeated, galvanised again. '*Must* go, Fanny!'

Reluctantly, Fanny got up off her bed. 'You've got a guilt complex, you have,' she said. 'All right. Come on, then.'

They went downstairs and past the sitting room where Matthew and Dominic sat before a deafening television set.

'Turn that *down*!' yelled Fanny as she closed the door behind Bobbie. 'And somebody come and help me in the kitchen!'

Neither of her brothers moved.

Bobbie dreaded facing the scene her mother would no doubt make but she wanted to hear the trumpet player again. And so, although she was already late, she took the longer way home so that she would pass the warehouse where the Brethren lived on her way to cross the railway bridge. She paused outside the brick building and looked up at the windows, but there was no music to be heard. Instead there came a very normal chatter of voices, both adults' and children's, and some rattling sounds which could have been saucepans or cutlery. Disappointed, Bobbie moved on – and was at once embarrassed to find that her pause had been watched by a young man standing in the warehouse doorway. He was dressed in jeans, dirty plimsolls and a monkey jacket and his fair, wavy hair fell from a centre parting to his shoulders. He came close to Bobbie, unsmiling but with his hands extended in a gesture of kindness.

'God loves you,' he told her gravely.

Does He? The words rose in Bobbie's mind, but she did not speak them. For a moment she stared at the young man, half fascinated and half afraid; then he returned to the doorway and went inside. Bobbie swung round and took a breath to call out, 'Does He?' – but the door had swung shut and she was alone in the street. She walked on quickly, along the alleyway that led to the bridge, hot with shame. Fanny would have had an answer ready at once, she reflected. How stupid to have been so tongue-tied. If only it could happen all over again, she might strike up a wonderful friendship with the trumpet player ... they would go to America, to New Orleans ... concerts, dances, television appearances, 'I have to have my wife with me wherever I go – she is my inspiration and my comfort, my whole life....'

Bobbie glanced back. The sides of the alleyway were high and she could no longer see the warehouse. She knew, with depressing certainty, that if it happened all over again, she would still not have the courage to speak.

Fanny's father drove his car into the garage and switched off the ignition with a sigh of relief. He'd had quite enough for one day. He went into the house, dropped his bag into the consulting room and shut the door on it. He could hear voices in the kitchen.

'Hello, Stewart!' said Fanny as he went in. 'Chicken pie!'

'Oh – good.' Stewart sat down in the rocking chair which he disliked because it rocked, and watched his daughter as she hacked negligently at a cold chicken, separating meat from bones with faint distaste. She wore flared jeans and a mud-coloured T-shirt with some kind of hairy sleeveless garment over it. Was it a very long waistcoat? Stewart wondered – or perhaps a jacket without sleeves? Whatever it was, it gave Fanny the appearance of slightly ludicrous beauty which all young women seemed to have these days.

Could she really be the same girl who had come yawning down to breakfast this morning, tie adrift, white shirt half buttoned and bare thighs as pink as bacon under the short navy skirt? How ridiculous these schools were to try and make young women look like soldiers. Who in their right mind would make any girl wear a *tie*, to start with? The female neck and shoulder construction simply wasn't suited to it.

'Matthew,' said Fanny, 'can you get me the pie dish? Under the work top, near the plates. And Dominic, be a dear and find a tin of mushrooms. In the cellar, I think.'

Matthew raised his eyebrows at Stewart in a gesture of long-suffering male complicity but went to get the pie dish. Dominic, on the other hand, gave no sign of having heard Fanny speak. He was constructing something of unknown function, using a polystyrene supermarket tray, a thick rubber band, a model aeroplane propeller and a large roll of Sellotape in addition to a tinful of assorted small objects. It was, inevitably, Matthew who went in search of the tinned mushrooms.

Stewart's twin sons had very little in common beyond an identical date of birth. Matthew was bigger than Dominic, more easy-going and open-minded, lacking Dominic's ferocious powers of concentration which, Stewart sometimes thought wryly, were clearly inherited from their mother. For Helen had a single-minded and persistent purposefulness which usually prevailed over all opposition. Stewart remembered, not without a certain bitterness, how she had argued with him during Fanny's last year at primary school, insisting that Critchlowe's was the only school strict enough to produce good academic results. Stewart had pointed out that human beings are not made to function purely as thinking machines. A complete person needed to develop in many different directions, he contended. But, Helen had objected, Fanny might never get to university from a comprehensive school.

Fanny doesn't want to go to university, Stewart had said. Fanny wants to go on the stage. Helen had laughed. And Helen, as always, had won.

Sylvia Rippon went to the mirror-lined cocktail cabinet and poured herself a sweet Cinzano. After a moment's pause, she added a slightly more than equal quantity of gin. She did not put a cherry in it, however. She was much too worried about Bobbie. There might be a policeman at the door at any minute to tell her of her daughter's death and it would seem so frivolous to be found drinking a cocktail with a cherry in it.

Helen's key scratched in the lock. 'Hello!' she called, and

came into the kitchen, depositing on the counter top her gloves and handbag, followed by a small pile of books and a lettuce in a damp brown paper bag. 'Oh, Fanny you *are* a good girl, doing the pie,' she said. 'Let's have a sherry, Stewart. Where's the pastry?' She put on a blue striped butcher's apron, crossing its long strings behind her and knotting them at her waist. She washed her hands at the sink, dried them on a briskly torn-off length of paper kitchen roll, took a sip of sherry and sprinkled flour on the pastry board.

'Have you ever read *Peter Pan*, Fanny?'

'Good Lord, no – except when I was tiny, I suppose. Why?'

'You must talk to Sandie McIver about it – Colin says she's reading it. She seems to think the Darlings are all psychopaths.'

'An author who calls his characters the Darlings *must* have made them psychopaths,' said Fanny.

'Oh, bitchy! Have you had a nasty day, darling? Or mustn't I call you darling?'

'I've had a *horrible* day,' said Fanny. 'That beastly woman took my play script.'

'Which particular beastly woman is that?' asked Stewart.

'Miss Perkins. She was doing simultaneous quadratics on the board and I know how to do those so I was learning my part with my fingers in my ears and she came and snatched it.'

'I should think so, too,' said Helen. 'It's very rude, reading in someone's lesson. Mental truancy.'

'But it was my property!' cried Fanny. 'OK, take it away in her lesson if she had to, but she shouldn't just *keep* it. I went to the staff room to ask her for it but she'd gone off home.'

'School is for work,' said Helen.

Fanny shook her head irritably. 'School is for *me*! Look, they're not raising future graduates like a farmer raises cattle, Helen! They don't sell us at the end! It's *us* that goes on and takes a place in the world, not them!'

Helen prodded crossly at the chicken and mushroom mixture in the pie dish. It was not going to be enough. 'Nip down and see if there's another tin of mushrooms, Matthew,' she said. Matthew sighed, but went.

'I think that's sheer self-centredness,' she said. 'I've just had a similar kind of argument with Colin, who thinks he's got the right to say exactly what he likes to people. What's the matter with you all these days? Me, me, sacred me! *Why* do you consider yourselves exempt from all forms of discipline? Why—'

'Not *all* forms.'

'– Why do you think you're so colossally important? You're no more important than we were at your age.'

'Of *course* we're not!' shouted Fanny. 'The only difference is that you didn't *realise* that you were important! You did as you were told, you got filled up with knowledge like pots of fish paste, you never questioned anything – if you had an original idea they told you not to be arrogant, same as they tell us, so you just forgot it, like a good little girl. And here you are, solid obedient citizens who won't let me go to drama school. Ugh!'

'Sounds as if you don't need to,' observed Stewart with a grin. Helen, however, was sparkling with anger. 'How dare you!' she said to Fanny. 'You may not realise it now, but the education you are getting will serve you well through your whole life. And if you're going to be personally abusive, I'd be glad if you'd leave the room.'

'Delighted,' said Fanny. She dusted her hands together elaborately and walked to the door, where she turned. 'You can *manage* a chicken pie, can you?' she inquired – and swept out.

Matthew came in, grinning. 'She's in one of her moods,' he said. 'I couldn't find any more mushrooms so I brought a tin of peas instead. Will that do?'

Helen did not answer so Stewart nodded at him encouragingly. 'That'll do fine,' he said, and took another sip of sherry.

Dominic carefully uncurled a paper clip and fixed it in place to represent a sonic detector device. 'I think *I'm* important,' he ventured. But nobody answered.

It had been a good exit line, thought Fanny. 'You can *manage* a chicken pie?' It had a nice rhythm. Went well with the turn at the door.

She sighed. She had not meant to quarrel with Helen in personal terms. It was the educational system which Fanny had intended to attack; how, then, had she managed to turn it into a squabble with her mother?

Fanny decided, with a sudden flash of inspiration, that it was all the fault of the English language. The word 'you' was employed to mean anything from a specific person to a generalised idea. But then, English had been saddled with such a cumbrous second-person form of address; 'thee' – 'thou' – too slow by half for modern speech rhythms. Why couldn't we have shortened it to 'ee', like West Country people and stage pirates?

'Do 'ee tap the brandy carsk, Jake,' said Fanny aloud, leering at her image in the mirror. Then, with some reluctance, she stopped leering and got out her physics homework. She had done her Latin during the English lesson and her geography during the lunch hour, so physics was all that remained. There should be enough time to finish that while the chicken pie was in the oven.

Fresh air, thought Colin as he walked home from the bookshop, was pretty difficult to find in this town. Although it was windy tonight, and damp, it was still soft and flavourless. All the same, he was lucky to be working in a bookshop. If they'd stayed in Scotland he'd most likely have been packing chickens at the processing plant.

It had been a bad move at that time, though, coming south when he was in the sixth form. His parents had been terrific about letting him stay on – God knows they could have done with the money he'd have earned – but the school down here was so different. They seemed – kids, somehow. And he was a big joke. Until he'd managed to modify his Dundee accent, everyone had fallen about with amusement when he spoke. Hoots McHairy and that sort of thing.

Colin turned down the alleyway that led to the footbridge, still mulling over his unsatisfactory school career. It had all seemed patchy and disconnected somehow, and by the time he'd got it organised again, the exams had come and gone and his three A-level passes were not good ones. Not good enough for university, anyway.

He climbed the steps to the narrow footbridge. Black steel arches spanned it like the skeleton of a tunnel. It was a long bridge, crossing the railway near its terminus, where it fanned out into the delta of a shunting yard. Colin liked the railway because it evoked the flavour of steam-age adventuring, the time of the great Victorians. He often felt that he should have been born a hundred years ago, when he could have taken a ship from Dundee with the jute men and gone to India. Had it really been as they said, with river parties in the scented nights and a mongoose in every house to kill the cobras? Oh, why had he missed the great days of the silk-clad mem-sahibs? How magnificently strong, how female, how imperious those women must have been, who not only endured the tropical heat, but endured it with their bodies encased in whalebone corsets! Pin-tucked and impeccable, they ran their households, gave orders to their servants, attended durbars, rode elephants, shot tigers and took tea with ranees exquisite in saris and silver jewellery. So magnificently dignified were these ladies that the punkah-wallah who pulled the string to wave the palm-leaf fan above their heads on the hot verandah was hidden behind a screen. 'Faster, boy!' they would call, dealing another hand of Bezique. 'Faster!'

Colin stood staring down at the railway lines, his mind crowded with the images of his dream land. Ayahs, pi-dogs, peacock feathers, sandalwood ... a train rattled by below him. He watched it slide into the station and stop, then he turned to continue on his way – and collided with the totally unexpected presence of another person.

The girl gasped and flung up an arm to keep her balance.

Colin grabbed at her, afraid that she would fall.

'I'm terribly sorry,' he said. 'Did I hurt you?'

The girl peered at him in the dim light of the single bulb on the arch above them.

'Colin?'

Her face was familiar, Colin realised. Wasn't she a friend of his sister, Sandie's? That's it, they were in the same form. With a struggle, he recalled her name.

'Bobbie!' he said triumphantly. 'Bobbie Rippon!'

'I'm terribly sorry,' said Colin again. 'I really am. Are you sure you're all right? Let me carry your basket for you.'

Bobbie relinquished the basket gladly. 'It's a bit heavy,' she warned him. 'Full of books.'

'I'm well used to *them*,' said Colin. 'I work in a bookshop.'

'Do you? In Smith's?'

'No, no,' said Colin, with a touch of distaste, 'it's a specialist children's bookshop called Jackanapes.'

'Oh, Mrs Anthony's shop! Fanny's mother!'

'That's right.'

'Fanny's my best friend. I've been at her house, actually – that's why I'm so late. We were writing horoscopes.'

'Horoscopes?'

'*You* know – all the magazines have one. "Your Stars This Week" and that sort of thing. We did really horrible ones for all the people we don't like.'

Colin smiled politely. 'Great,' he said. Bobbie blushed.

'Well, I know it sounds awfully stupid but – well, we thought it was fun.'

'I'm sorry,' said Colin, irritated to find himself in the wrong again. 'I didn't say it wasn't fun.'

'I know.'

They left the bridge and turned into Oswald Road, walking in silence.

'Your sister's just the same,' Bobbie tried to explain. 'It's not that she hasn't got a sense of humour because she has, but – I don't know, she's sort of *serious*.' She laughed suddenly. 'She put her hand up once when our form teacher was going on and on about something silly, and said, "Excuse me, Mrs Newley, but do you really consider that the subject under discussion is worthy of the amount of time we are spending on it?" We all fell about.'

'It sounds quite a reasonable thing to say.'

'That's just it. Mrs Newley was furious but she couldn't say anything because Sandie was looking so serious and responsible.'

'What *was* the subject under discussion, anyway?'

'Oh, whether we should be allowed to wear hair ribbons any other colour except black or white. There was no point in talking about it because we're not. It's a rule.'

'Heaven preserve us!' said Colin in disbelief.

They turned out of Oswald Road into Orchard Walk, where Bobbie lived.

'You're hurrying,' said Colin.

'Am I? Sorry. Actually, I *am* a bit late, though, and my mother gets awfully worried.'

Colin lengthened his stride. He was beginning to feel very attracted to this girl with her crazy mop of hair and her long, slim legs. Her big eyes and pointed chin made her look like a cat, he thought. Not a fluffy, persian cat, though – a small, wild, jungle cat. How old was she? Fifteen, of course, same as Sandie. Or thereabouts.

'Listen,' he said, 'd'you ever go out with anyone? Pictures or anything?'

She did not answer at once, but continued to walk very fast, her hands jammed deep in her blazer pockets. Colin was suddenly angry.

'Look, don't be so blasted coy, Bobbie! If you've got a boyfriend, just say so and I won't mind, and if you haven't, then d'you want to come out with me or not?'

Bobbie stopped with a gasp and turned to face him. 'You don't have to be so beastly!' she said, 'I *wasn't* being coy. If you must know, I've never been out with any boy and I was just thinking what I'd have to say to my mother, that's all. I'm *sorry*.'

Contrite, Colin put his hand on her arm. 'My fault,' he said. 'McIver puts his foot in it again. Gosh, I've known you ten minutes and I've had to apologise three times already. No wonder you don't want to see me.'

'But I do!' The words were out almost before Bobbie had intended them and Colin's hand was still on her arm.

'You do? Oh, that's great! When? Tomorrow?'

'It's difficult during the week because of the homework. It's set one day for the next, you see, so I can't ever leave it for the next night.'

'Saturday, then. Or Friday. What about this Friday?' They were walking on again, companionably, Colin's hand tucked under Bobbie's elbow.

'Friday would be super – but I'll have to tell them at home. Look, this is where I live. You'd better give me my basket back.'

'OK. Friday, then. What time?'

Before Bobbie could answer, the front door of the house was flung open and her mother rushed down the path towards them.

'Bobbie! Oh, Bobbie, I've been so *worried*!' She stopped short when she saw Colin. 'So *that's* what you've been doing!' Her voice changed to a thick, angry shout. 'Here's me been half out of my mind – I was just going to ring the *police* about you, d'you realise that? – and all the time you're hanging about, picking up *men*. My daughter. Out at night, picking up *men*.'

'It's only six o'clock, Mrs Rippon,' said Colin reasonably.

'Ten past,' snapped Sylvia. 'And don't you talk to me, you – you – whoever you are. You can just damn well shut up, that's what you can do. And go away, too. That's it.' She was almost incoherent, her speech slurred. 'Yes, go away. Bobbie, come inside!'

'In a minute,' said Bobbie. 'Go indoors, Mum. I'll be in in a minute.'

For a moment Colin thought Mrs Rippon was going to attack Bobbie, but she turned and made her way unsteadily back to the house, where she leaned dramatically against the doorpost, her head buried in her arms. Quite clearly, she was very drunk.

'Well,' said Bobbie, with a weary hardness in her voice which surprised Colin, 'that's my mother. It's because I'm late, you see, and she's been alone. Do you still want to take me out?'

Colin grasped her by the shoulders and gave her a small, gentle shake. 'Don't be so daft,' he said. 'It's *you* I want to see, not your mother.' It could not be ignored, though. 'Look – is she like this often? I mean, she's hit the bottle pretty hard. Will you be all right?'

'Oh, I'll be all right,' said Bobbie tiredly. 'It doesn't happen all that often and she's quite different usually. Colin – you won't tell anyone, will you? Nobody else knows – not even Fanny, because she doesn't come here much. If Fanny knew she'd want to *do* something. And that would be awful.'

Colin nodded, a little doubtfully. 'Well, if you're sure.'

'You won't tell Mrs Anthony?'

'I won't tell Mrs Anthony. But look, Bobbie – if you ever need any help, will you promise to tell me? We're on the phone and we live not too far away, in Manor Street. Number thirty-seven. Can you remember that?'

'Thirty-seven Manor Street.'

'You could come any time. My parents are all right, they wouldn't mind.'

'There's Sandie.'

'She's quite sensible, you said so yourself. She wouldn't gossip.'

'Perhaps not. Look, I'd better go.'

'What time on Friday? Seven?'

'That would be fine.'

'Bye, then. And remember, just let me know.'

'I will. Bye-bye. Oh, Colin – thanks!'

He gave her one of his rare smiles. 'It's a very real pleasure,' he said. Bobbie smiled back. Then, picking up her basket of books, she turned and walked up the path, towards the house and her mother.

Sylvia Rippon pounded the polished surface of the table, four or five times. 'I wanted you to be *good*,' she said thickly. 'Really – *good*. You're my daughter. My creation.'

'There's Marjorie as well,' said Bobbie. 'She's your daughter, too.'

'Marjorie! What's Marjorie ever done? Wouldn't try for medical school, settled for being a dental nurse. Mixing up muck to push into people's rotten old teeth. *My daughter.*'

'But she's happy,' persisted Bobbie. 'She's a good nurse. She makes people feel at ease; she does a good job. And she married Gordon. You like Gordon.'

'A *car* salesman,' moaned Sylvia. 'It's all so degrading. There's nothing to *admire*. I won't accept these compromises. Everything is so second rate.'

Bobbie sighed. This was a familiar refrain. 'What's for supper?' she asked. Her mother made a dismissive gesture as though to imply that supper was too squalid a matter even to contemplate – and at that moment they both heard David Rippon's car turn into the drive.

Sylvia dashed up the stairs and, almost before her father had come into the room, Bobbie could hear water splashing in the bathroom as her mother set about making her face look presentable.

'Hello,' said David, tossing his evening newspaper on to the table. 'Where's your mother?'

'Upstairs,' said Bobbie. Her father looked at her narrowly and went across to the cocktail cabinet. The Cinzano bottle was empty and the gin very depleted. He levered the top off a bottle of beer, poured it carefully into a glass and sat down.

'Well, Fanny, if you really need this script,' said Helen during dinner, all rancour forgotten, 'why don't you go round to the Theatre Centre and see if they've got a spare one?'

'I think I will,' said Fanny. 'I've done all my homework. Is there any more pie?'

'I'll want some,' said Dominic warningly.

Helen shared out the last of the pie, which was of a rather curious texture, since she had finally had to resort to thickening a can of mushroom soup in order to fill the pie dish to a reasonable level.

Fanny pushed her chair back. 'Shan't be long,' she said.

Some minutes later, Stewart glanced up from his newspaper. 'Where's Fanny gone?' he asked.

'To the Theatre Centre,' Helen told him patiently. Matthew grinned and Dominic continued to peruse the reverse side of his father's newspaper. They all knew that the necessity to pay attention to people was, as far as Stewart was concerned, a technique which belonged with all his other professional apparatus, in his consulting room.

Fanny enjoyed being out in the dark. The houses were so much less boring when they lurked sinisterly in the shadows. People were like that, too; terribly dull in the daytime but much more romantic at night. Perhaps, Fanny thought, that's why she loved the theatre so much – because of the bright lights that made everything a little strange. And yet the unreality of the stage was more real than the people out there in the dark auditorium – that hot, shuffly corporate animal called an audience.

Fanny gave a little shiver of excitement. Going to the Theatre Centre always made her feel excited although the place was nothing more than a converted Victorian house. She quickened her pace and passed the last three houses at a run.

Mary Ross had lingered long and luxuriously in her bath and she emerged from the bathroom feeling not merely better but positively good. Lee Haynes, who was crossing the landing on his way up to his room, gaped. He had often imagined meeting a very pretty girl coming out of a bathroom in a state of slight undress and Mary, wafted by a cloud of scented steam, was a dream come true. She wore a floor-length dressing gown of which, Lee noticed with regret, only the sleeves were transparent. She clutched an armful of miscellaneous bathing gear and her hair, pinned on top of her head to keep it dry, drooped a curl here and there in a most stimulatingly undressed kind of way.

'Hel-*lo*!' said Lee. 'Well – well – well! You our new girl, are you?' Mary gave him a fleeting smile and continued her way across the landing.

'Can't I carry something for you?' asked Lee. 'Lend you some sugar? Share my pint of milk?'

'No, thank you.'

A shift of approach was needed. 'No, seriously,' said Lee, looking honest and responsible, 'if I can help with anything – I mean, fix anything electrical, shift the furniture – anything like that – just give a shout. I'm in the top floor back.'

Mary, who came from an academic family whose males were totally incompetent when it came to the practical things of life, had a weakness for handy men.

'That's awfully kind of you,' she said. 'The wiring here *does* seem a bit funny. I was thinking of getting a toaster but—'

'Lovely,' said Lee. 'Nothing like a spot of hot buttered in the morning. Just you let me know and I'll put a plug on it for you, supplied free by yours truly. I'm a television fitter, see. Plugs fall off the backs of lorries the whole time in our trade. Never know – I might even come across a toaster that's looking for a good home. Save you a quid or two.'

'Oh, but I wouldn't want you to—'

Lee held up his hand masterfully. 'Say no more!' He moved a step closer. She smelled beautiful. 'Tell you what I think,' he said earnestly, 'I think the only way any of us are going to get better kind of lives is if we all help each other. Share what we've got to offer. Don't you?' He gave her his slightly diffident look, serious but lacking in confidence. It worked beautifully.

'Oh, I do!' she said. And she smiled at him warmly, all hostility melted away by his honesty.

'I'll drop in a bit later, then,' pursued Lee, 'with a screwdriver. Just give that wiring the once-over. OK?'

'That *would* be kind,' said Mary. 'I'll make some coffee.'

'Great,' said Lee. And, having won the opening game, he offered her the freedom of the stairs with a courtly sweep of his arm. 'After you!'

'Thank you,' said Mary, gathering up the skirt of her dressing gown. Lee followed her up the stairs. She had smashing legs.

'Have another sausage!' said Sylvia Rippon gaily, waving the serving tongs. With fresh makeup, she had put on frivolity. Life, for Sylvia, was a series of new starts.

'No, thanks,' said David shortly.

'Bobbie?'

Bobbie shook her head dumbly. She could not play the gaiety game. Tonight she wanted to be quiet, so that she could think about her meeting with Colin. He had seemed so strong and so comforting. And so gentle.

'Oh, come on, Dave,' coaxed Sylvia. 'They're smashing sossies! The ones you like. All pork. Real cordon bleu bangers!' She smiled at him, head on one side, but this time he did not respond.

Abruptly, Sylvia's face changed. She flung the serving tongs down on the dish. 'All right!' she shouted. 'Just bloody *be* like that! You know the trouble with you? You're jealous of me – just jealous! Because you look middle-aged and I don't, because I'm *alive* – because I *feel* and you don't know what feeling is! You wouldn't *mind* being shut in this house, would you, worrying and worrying about your tarty little daughter hanging round with all the riff-raff of the district! Oh, no, you wouldn't think about that, would you, all you'd hear is tick, tick, tick, because you're just a bloody, inhuman computer!' And she swept out of the room.

'Shit,' said David. He turned on his daughter savagely. 'Now look what you've done! What d'you want to go and upset her for? How d'you think I like it, coming back to a house full of screaming women when I've been working hard all day?'

The injustice of the attack left Bobbie speechless. A dozen defences rushed to her mind. She had given no provocation and done nothing wrong except to meet Colin and that was entirely by accident. What's more, she had been almost super-humanly patient with her drunken, embarrassing mother. Christ, Dad, she protested in silent words, she's *your* wife, not mine. And Colin *isn't* riff-raff. This last thought was the one which penetrated her almost exhausted defences and threatened her with tears. She leaned her head on her hand, trying to hide her face, but the burning tightness in her throat grew and grew. She stared at the half-eaten sausage in its little mess of tinned spaghetti on her plate, and fought to re-establish normality, but the unwanted forlornness of the sausage added a dreadful poignancy of its own. Blindly, she pushed her chair back and bolted to the haven of her room.

'Bloody women!' shouted her father as she slammed the door. He continued to shout for some time but Bobbie, chok-ing with sobs as she lay face down on her bed, pulled the pillow over her head so that she could not hear him.

Fanny pushed open the red-painted door of the Theatre Centre and went in. The corridor ahead of her led to a flight of stairs at the top of which were the dressing rooms, ward-robe, workshops and all the other paraphernalia of a theatre. To Fanny's left, black baize-covered doors gave access to a small auditorium. On her right was the Green Room and kitchen. The cupboard under the stairs became a Box Office during performances and then Mrs Lovelace would sit framed in its sloping-topped doorway, her tickets arranged before her on a trestle table. Tonight, however, there was no performance. The Senior Group would be opening with *The Knight of the Burning Pestle* next week and *Us Lot* was cast and ready to go into rehearsal as the next production.

Through the auditorium doors, Fanny could hear the high-pitched quacking of Felicity Percival as the Citizen's Wife.

None of the people she was looking for would be involved in that production, so Fanny went into the Green Room.

Low benches ran round the wall – a relic of the days when the house had been used as a small private school and this had been a cloakroom. At one end of the room was a bar; at the other a large hatch and a door beside it communicated with the kitchen. Tonight, to Fanny's disappointment, the place was empty except for a group of younger members who sprawled and giggled in the armchairs which they had pulled together cosily in the middle of the room. Empty Coke bottles littered the floor beside them. The kitchen hatch was up but nobody presided at the counter, although a subdued cloud of steam issued from the kettle on its turned-down gas.

Fanny collected the Coke bottles. 'You might tidy up after you,' she said rather censoriously.

'We would have done,' said one of the boys. 'But you got here first – Miss.'

The 'Miss' stung Fanny a little, as it was meant to do. Schoolmarm Fanny Anthony, the boy had implied. Old bossy-boots. Crossly, she carried the bottles into the kitchen and put them in the crate under the sink. There were a few dirty coffee cups on the draining board so she stacked them into a washing bowl and turned on the Ascot.

From outside, she heard the squeak of chairs and scuff of feet as the boys and girls got up to go. 'Goodnight!' she called. ''Night, Fanny!' they shouted back. ''Night, Ken!'

Ken! A tingle ran down Fanny's back. Ken was here!

Ken Olliphant, who ran the Junior Section, came into the kitchen. He was a tall, broad man, whose round face habitually wore an easy-going smile. He was dressed in a white polo-necked sweater, jeans and dirty plimsolls which, combined with the tonsure-like bald patch on the top of his head, made him look like a renegade Franciscan friar. Ken had turned his ludicrous name into an asset. In his early days as a student teacher he had developed what he termed 'the Olliphantine manner' and this had now become an unconscious style. The unhurried, soft-footed walk, the easy smile and the bland

refusal to be chivvied into taking unconsidered action all combined to give the impression of relaxed, infinitely good-
natured joviality. Everybody adored Ken Olliphant, but Fanny
had felt for a long time that she adored him – yes, and understood him – far more deeply than anyone else could.

'Hello, Fan,' said Ken. 'Mrs Lovelace land you with the
coffee, did she?'

Fanny looked blank.

'Obviously not,' Ken answered his own question. 'No, the
daft old baggage was going to do the coffee for yonder
thespians' (he was always sarcastic about the Senior Group,
who were not his concern) 'but then she couldn't. Crunge of the
knees or something. And, finding you here, up to the pretty
elbows in soap suds, I thought the lot, so to speak, had fallen
on you.'

'Oh, I see,' said Fanny. 'Well, I don't mind doing coffee for
them now I'm here. But I really came to see if anyone had a
spare script.'

'Where's yours?'

'Impounded for learning it in maths. The thing is, I don't
know if I'll get it back. She doesn't like me.'

Ken rolled his eyes. 'She must be mad!' he declared passionately, then added, 'But really, Fan, I hope you *do* get it back,
because I'm awfully short of scripts. That's the trouble with
unpublished plays, you see, trying to get hold of enough copies.
You have to seek the favours of the school secretary and our
lovely lady guards the key of her Gestetner as though it
unlocked her chastity belt. Costs me a mint of money in choco-
lates, she does.'

Fanny giggled, prodding with a dishmop at the crystallised
sugar in the bottom of a cup. 'Your school sounds much more
fun than ours,' she said. 'I suppose it's because you're comprehensive. Ours is grim.'

'Ah,' said Ken with a knowing sideways nod, ' "Male and
female created He them" – or words to that effect. Silly idea,
separating the sexes. Makes it so difficult to cast the school
play, apart from anything else. You fetch up with some first-

year lad squeaking, "unhand me, Sir Henry" with two tennis balls down his bodice.'

'They'd be *horrified* at school if anyone said that! About the tennis balls, I mean. They'd think it was really vulgar.'

'So it is. So what?'

'Well—' The gulf was so immense that Fanny felt at a loss as to how to define it. 'You see, we all do human biology right through the first year and after that nobody ever mentions anything to do with sex. It's as if they think "there, that's got *that* out of their systems".'

'It's my belief,' said Ken, 'that you exaggerate a bit, my lovely. Nobody can talk about Shakespeare without referring to sex, for a start. It's one of life's great fundamentals. Good Lord, the French even incorporate it into their language and so do the Germans and the Italians and God knows who else. Only they call it gender. I suppose that makes it all much nicer.'

'Oh, yes, that's different altogether. But Mrs Newley says all other languages are inferior to English. Isn't that funny, considering she teaches French? She's a great one for making large statements of that sort. She had a great spiel the other day about how one should bring up boys and I don't know what *she* knows about it – she hasn't got any kids at all, let alone boys!'

Ken grinned. 'Sounds as if I'd better keep my mouth shut,' he said. 'My second go at being a husband packed up two years ago and the kids went with their mother so—' he shrugged. 'No large statements.'

Fanny was suddenly overwhelmed with pity and fury. She was also, in some complex way, deeply shocked. Ken, of all people, had always seemed so calm and happy – so normal. What woman could possibly have treated him so badly? How could she have been so unappreciative? Ken would be such a lovely person to live with and sleep with – such a gorgeous father for one's children.... Fanny rattled the cups about busily in the bowl, realising to her intense annoyance that a blush had spread over her face because her thoughts had caught her unawares. She stood the last two cups upside down on the wooden rack above the sink and turned the water out of the bowl too fast, so that she had to jump out of the way of the splashes.

'There we are!' she said, over-briskly. 'Now – how many is it for coffee?'

'Fifteen.' Ken eyed her. Fanny had always seemed to be such a cool cookie but now her confusion was obvious.

'Milk?' Fanny still did not look at him, busy mopping round the sink with a dish cloth.

'There's only powdered. And Mrs Stackhouse likes hers black. Bleck,' he repeated in a heavy German accent, 'mit seffen Seccherines!'

He was relieved to see Fanny smile. Perhaps he shouldn't have mentioned his divorce ... no, that couldn't be it. Fanny had her feet on the ground all right. Nothing if not a realist. Probably nuts about some boyfriend or other. Lucky chap.

'Come to think of it, Fan, Lee Haynes has got a script. He's doing the lights as usual and I gave him a script for cues but he won't need it until we go into rehearsal. So what about borrowing his? I'll run you up there if you like – bit of a drag to walk it.'

The thought of being alone with Ken in his car was appealing but Fanny shook her head, feeling far too uncertain. 'It's hardly worth it,' she said. 'I wouldn't have time to learn any tonight, not if I'm going to do the Seniors' coffee. No, I'll just have to *make* Miss Perkins give mine back tomorrow.'

'That's the stuff,' said Ken. 'Or warn her that wild Olliphants will drag it from her.'

This was one of Ken's oldest jokes, but it still made Fanny laugh.

'Well,' said Lee, as Mary rather pointedly cleared away the cups, 'I'll say goodnight, then. Thanks for the coffee.'

Mary smiled. 'Oh, that's nothing. I'm very grateful for the insulating tape. I'd never have known those wires were actually *dangerous*.'

Dangerous, hell, thought Lee. 'Never can tell!' he said. 'And I'll have a look round for a toaster, shall I?'

'Would you? It's awfully kind of you. I say....'

'M'm?'

'I do hope I wasn't an awful bore, chatting on about school. It just – you know – got on top of me a bit and it's so nice to have someone to talk to. It sort of clears the mind.'

'Any time!' said Lee gallantly, raising the roll of insulating tape in a smart salute. 'Goodnight!'

'Goodnight.' Mary remained firmly out of reach, smiled at him very nicely – and closed the door. It was as calm and adroit as if she had never thought of Lee as a normally lusty man at all. Maybe, Lee thought as he mounted the stairs to his own room, she hadn't. But he wouldn't give up. Not yet.

Colin McIver, sitting in the front room with his father and his sisters Sandie and Nicola, heard the gentle thump of his mother's feet as she padded about in the room overhead, settling little Ian in his cot. Colin felt extremely restless. Meeting Bobbie this evening had left him in a state of mental and physical uneasiness and he stared unseeingly at the twittering television set. To his slight shame, he found that the warm, soft girl he kept leading up the stairs of his mind to bed was not necessarily Bobbie. She had no face except prettiness, no hair except scentedness, no body except eagerness. And then, with a conscious effort, Colin managed to see Bobbie's face in his mind's eye. He was aware again of her wild halo of dark hair and her small cat-mouth, and he decided that it really was Bobbie he wanted. Very much wanted.

'Are you watching this seriously?' asked Sandie. 'Because I want to change over.'

'Me, too,' said Nicola. 'It's that thing about the mother and the father and two children.'

'Sounds fascinating,' said Colin sarcastically.

'Well, why do you sit there if you don't want to watch it?' asked Sandie. 'Nobody's forcing you to.'

Colin jumped to his feet. 'I'm going out,' he said.

'Where to?' asked Sandie.

Mr McIver put his paper down and looked at her reprovingly. 'Let your brother alone,' he said. 'If he's going out, he's going out. No need for him to be accountable to you or anyone else at his age. Just remember you've a job to be going to in the morning, Colin, eh?' He returned his attention to the girls. 'Now, change the programme if you want to and let's have less of this silliness.'

He gave Colin a dismissive but friendly nod. Unnatural for a lad of his age to be cooped up in a small room with a television set, he considered. High time he was out with the lassies.

Colin felt much better once he was outside the house. He walked fast, down the road and then, turning left, along the railway path that led to the footbridge where he had met Bobbie. He crossed the bridge, ran through the alleyway and turned into Wilmot Road, then went on walking until he came to the unmade roads which ran between the wide areas of playing fields.

This was Colin's favourite part of the town. It was no substitute for real farm land but at least there were no buildings and the sky was empty. The wind blew freshly across the flat land and the rain-puddled gravel roads smelt sharp and earthy. The privet hedges, too, held a faint aroma of wet leaves and there was an all-pervading reek of mud from the boot-churned football pitches.

On a Saturday night there would have been cars parked all the way along the gravel roads and lights would have been blazing in every clubhouse – but this was a Monday. A gleam of light showed here and there from a committee room or a groundsman's flat but otherwise the landscape was dark and silent. Colin thought wistfully of Dundee. There were so many places there which he knew well; so many friends to drink with and walk through the streets with; so many different things to do. There was nothing here but rows and rows of suburban houses.

The houses were too important, Colin thought. People

51

stayed inside them like snails inside their shells. He had read somewhere that there is a species of marine snail which decorates its shell by sticking bits of weed on to it. No doubt if they were able to, they'd grow a privet hedge round it, he thought bitterly. The greater suburban mollusc. The trouble was that nobody worked here. All the men had jobs in London; they went away in crowded trains in the morning and came back, exhausted, in crowded trains in the evening, each one back to his little shell where they ate, grumbled, stared at the television, went to bed, had a little sex and slept. Family life. God preserve me, thought Colin, from family life. I would like a girl to be with me – I would like to marry her, even, if she felt it necessary. But the world is big and there are things to do and places to see, people to meet ... oh, God preserve me from the four walls and the television set.

A sudden rustle in the hedge followed by a slight but distinct flopping sound startled him and for an instant Colin stood rigidly still. Then he saw in the light from a street lamp that a large frog was sitting at his feet. It rotated a few degrees, pushing itself round with its hand-like front legs, then hopped lethargically away across the road. Colin followed it. There was something very pleasant about meeting a fellow-creature in this dark, empty place and besides, the frog had an independence which Colin admired. The frog stopped again and once more changed direction. This time it set off down the middle of the road, bouncing gravely along like a rubber ball which has become sticky in its old age.

Colin saw a light approaching – probably a bicycle – and realised that the frog was in considerable danger of being run over. He picked the frog up gently in both hands, and carried it over to the privet hedge which bordered the road. He found a gap big enough to put his arm through and, squatting down, put the frog through the hedge into the damp, unmown grass on the other side. It kicked sharply against his hands and leapt away out of sight in the darkness. Colin stayed in his squatting position, listening for any sign of the frog's return. Frogs, he had read, were becoming scarce because so many waterways were being drained or run through culverts underground or, if remaining open, were polluted to a point where they would not support life. This frog, at least, had a good chance of survival.

Bicycle tyres hissed on the gravel and stopped. There was a crunch as a heavy foot was set to the ground and a light bloomed suddenly, dazzling Colin as he instinctively looked round. He rose to his feet, shielding his eyes with his hand.

'Good evening, sir.' The voice unmistakably belonged to a policeman.

'Good evening,' said Colin. 'I do wish you'd put that light out.'

The light continued to shine steadily into his face.

'Out for a walk, are you, sir?'

Colin hated being called 'sir'. It made him feel certain that the man was being sarcastic although the voice was impeccably grave.

'Yes, I'm out for a walk.'

'Walk this way often, do you, sir?'

'Not very often.'

'Do you know whose property that is, the other side of the hedge?'

Colin shook his head, then added, 'No, I don't.'

The policeman considered him carefully. 'You're not from round these parts, are you, lad?'

'No.' 'Lad' was better than 'sir', Colin thought. Patronising, but less ominous.

'Scotch, are you?'

'Scottish,' corrected Colin. 'Yes. From Dundee. But we live here now.'

The policeman undid his tunic pocket and produced a notebook.

'Let's have your name, lad.'

'But why? I've done nothing wrong.'

'Your name, lad.'

'Colin McIver.'

'M-a-c or M-c capital I?'

'M-c capital I. But I don't see—'

'You don't have to see. Address?'

'Thirty-seven Manor Street. But—'

'Thirty – seven – Manor – Street,' the policeman repeated slowly as he wrote. Then he looked up. 'That the Manor Street by the railway?'

'Yes.'

'Live there with your parents?'

'Yes.'

'How long have you lived there?'

'Since we came from Scotland, about eighteen months.'

'Dundee, you said. What was your address in Dundee?'

'Fourteen, Blair Terrace. Look—'

'Got a job, have you?'

'Yes, I work in a bookshop.'

'What bookshop?'

'Does it matter?'

'*What* bookshop?'

'The children's bookshop in the High Street, if you must know. It's called Jackanapes and it's run by Mrs Helen Anthony and I've been there since I left school in the summer. Anything else?'

'Don't be cheeky, lad.' The policeman snapped his notebook shut and buttoned it back into his pocket. Then he again turned his torch beam on to Colin's face. 'All right. Now, suppose you tell me what you were doing down there by the hedge. Don't say you were out for a walk, because you weren't. You were crouching down.' The policeman deflected his torch from Colin's face, down to the place where he had been crouching, and inspected it for a moment or two as though hoping to see something significant there. He returned the beam to Colin's face – then switched it off.

'Come on, lad,' he said in the darkness. 'Let's have it. Giving the place the once-over, were you? Coming back later with your friends to see what you could find?'

'*No!*' Colin was furious. 'Most certainly not!'

'What, then? Waiting for a couple of girls to come along?

Nice dark road, m'm? Or better still, one on her own. Eh?'

The policeman's voice was almost cosy, inviting confidence. Colin stifled a wild desire to hit him. 'If you *must* know,' he said, tight-lipped with anger, 'I was putting a frog through the hedge.'

'A what?'

'A frog, man! F-R-O-G, *frog*!'

'No need to be rude, son.'

'No need?' Colin's Scottish sense of justice had been grievously offended. 'No need? Good Lord, you have my name, my address, my place of work, my employer – what more d'you want? I came out for a walk – and as far as I know there's no law against that – and I very nearly stepped on a frog and you may or may not know that there is alarm among naturalists about the dwindling number of frogs. So I picked it up and put it through the hedge so it shouldn't get trodden on or run over.' Colin flung out his arms in appeal. 'Now, what's the matter with that? What was I supposed to do? Tread on the frog? Or look round first to see that I wasn't being watched by a policeman? You tell me!'

Colin jutted out his chin aggressively, half-expecting the policeman to whistle up a paddy-wagon and bundle him off to the station. In Dundee the police meant business. No doubt they did here, too. But, to Colin's astonishment, the policeman merely chuckled comfortably as he hooked his flashlight back on to his belt. 'Well,' he said, 'I've heard some funny ones, but frogs!' He shook his head in amusement.

'I'm glad you think it's so funny,' said Colin, still smarting.

'We've got our job to do,' said the policeman, irritated with Colin for his lack of good sportsmanship. 'If you are fond of taking evening walks, sir, I would suggest that you frequent the better-lit parts of the town. Goodnight.'

He remounted his bicycle and rode away.

Face down on her bed, Bobbie Rippon cried and cried. It was like being sick; she could not stop crying any more than she could have stopped vomiting.

Was there no way out of this maze of misery? She thought of pleasant things, like summer holidays when she was a child – but nostalgia only sharpened her present bleakness. There had been lovely weekends then, when Daddy was at home, making kites for her to fly on the windy Common or pulling down the prickly bramble strands with a stick when they went blackberrying. But that was when they lived in the other house, the one with only three bedrooms.

She tried to think ahead to brighter times, but that was even more depressing. As far as Bobbie could see, there was absolutely nothing to look forward to. School consisted of a small pattern repeated again and again, classroom after classroom, teacher after teacher, cloakroom after plimsoll-smelling cloakroom. And coming home.... The thought of coming home caused Bobbie's throat to tighten again. Coming home always meant the making of an effort. Each day, it threatened to be a crisis. Sometimes her mother would be effusively maternal, guilt-stricken and loving, bubbling over with charm and humour. At others, she would be truculent and aggressive, raging against everyone, including herself, and at such times Bobbie would try to avoid speaking to her. No, coming home was not something to look forward to.

All that Bobbie could hope for was that something totally unexpected might happen; something like her meeting with Colin. Colin. That was another thing. She would have to tell her father that she had made a date with Colin, and there would undoubtedly be a serious row about it. Her father was a man who, above all, liked to be consulted.

Bobbie reached for another Kleenex and blew her nose noisily, feeling glad that her mother was not within earshot. 'Good God, girl,' Sylvia had once remarked acidly, 'you sound like a bloody trumpet.'

Trumpet. A trumpeter playing music in a warehouse and a trumpeter blowing a stuffy nose in a bedroom. Bobbie gave a giggle which turned into a sob. The music she had heard in the street had been so beautiful. 'God loves you.' The young man's grave assurance came back to Bobbie with a wistful bitterness.

Without much real hope, she wished that God did love her. She wished that someone or something could love her unconditionally and with total acceptance; that there existed a being who would demand nothing from her and to whom she need make no pretence; who would never say, as Fanny did, 'you *can't* believe that, Bobbie!' or, as her father did, 'why don't you bloody well *think*!' There is a green hill far away. Bare feet and the scent of grass and kind eyes filled with infinite understanding. Oh, Jesus Christ, love me.

Not for the first time, Bobbie wished that she could die. She had no desire to destroy herself, for she did not hate the person she was, but she felt deeply tired of the continual struggle. If death was like sleep, it would be so peaceful. Just an endless nothing.

Besides — Bobbie slipped easily into the familiar fantasy — her parents would be so sorry if she died. They would find her in the morning, her dark hair fanned out round her white face, still and cold. It would be late — it was always late — nearly quarter past eight as her father came barging into her room, shouting, 'Are you going to lie there all day?' Yes, oh, yes, Dad. All this day and all the days from now on, her silent voice would answer him. And Mum would come, tousle-haired from bed, holding her dressing gown round her with one hand, touching the cold face on the white pillow with the other — and then she would weep. 'Oh, my little girl, my lovely, my Bobbie. . . .'

How odd, Bobbie mused dully, that a part of her remained detached from all this misery. There seemed to be an essential awareness as small as a dot of light, that stayed unaffected while the rest of her was overwhelmed with distress. Was this tiny centre what the Christians called a soul? Could it really go on after death? It would be such a comfort to think that it did — that the long nothing led to some other state of lovely calmness.

Sleep suddenly blacked out Bobbie's mind. Fully clothed, her face red and swollen with tears, she breathed heavily through her mouth.

Because she was asleep, Bobbie did not hear the row which see-sawed from abuse to counter-abuse between her parents in the sitting room, and she did not hear the slam of the front door or the roar of the Jaguar as David left the house and drove away.

Colin was still angry when he came to Wilmot Road. He strode past the big houses and the chestnut trees until he came to the commercial end of the road near the station. The poor end, as he described it bitterly to himself. The working-class end. The end where the cops expect no protest when they pick up people for no reason. The blunt end of the stick. The thin end of the wedge.

The casual injustices of life infuriated Colin. He could not bring himself to accept them as his father did. 'That's the way things are, laddie.' Surely, he argued, to accept them was to condone them?

A boy of about Colin's own age came out of a doorway in one of the brick buildings, a letter in his hand.

'God loves you, brother,' he remarked as he passed. Colin swung round incredulously.

'God *what*?'

'God loves you.' The young man turned to face Colin. His reiteration was neither emphatic nor rude; neither was it merely a ritual greeting. He had made a statement. Colin frowned.

'How d'ye *know* He loves me?' he said, his Scottish accent more pronounced in his irritation.

'He died for you,' said the young man serenely. 'Would you die for someone you didn't love?'

'No, He didn't. I never asked anyone to die for me so why should I be grateful? It's not love at all, it's emotional black-mail. It's like these mothers who say "After all I've done for you" – it's just to make you feel guilty. I don't want *anyone* to die for me!'

'He lives for you, too,' said the young man, unruffled by

58

Colin's outburst. 'He lives in all of us, so we all live for each other. God is everywhere.'

'Oh, that's great.' Colin's temper rose. 'I suppose He divides this street into the posh end and the mucky end, does He? He tells the cops which ones to pick up and which to touch their caps to? Ach, ye make me sick.'

'It is good to be loved,' the young man persisted gently. Colin tried to bring his temper under control and organise his thoughts.

'Look,' he said, 'you can't have an exclusive contract on love! Everyone needs love, OK, but it's love between *people* we need, not some half-baked hot-line to a halo!'

'Love between people *is* God's love. He moves in us. It is His love that we feel.'

'Oh, rubbish! The Red Indians thought it was their God that put the rainbow in the sky, just because they didn't know about the prismatic effect of raindrops. It's the same with us – we invent God as a name for what we don't understand. It's a sort of cowardice. Finding someone to take the rap.'

Untroubled, the young man moved a few paces to the letter box at the edge of the pavement and dropped his letter in it, then returned to Colin. 'Come in,' he said, gesturing at the warehouse door. 'Come and witness God's love at work among us.'

Colin hovered. Curiosity tempted him but he recognised that, in his present mood, to go in would undoubtedly result in a full-scale quarrel. The thought of being preached at by a whole gang of Bible-punchers was more than he could put up with.

'Thanks,' he said, 'but it's a bit late and I've to be at work tomorrow.'

'Come another time, then. You are always welcome.'

'I might do that. Goodnight!'

'Goodnight. God bless you.' The young man turned and went through the door behind him, quiet on his plimsolled feet.

It had begun to rain, a light, insistent drizzle drifting finely through the patches of yellow light under the street lamps.

Colin turned up his collar and pushed his hands deep into his pockets. One of these days he would take up the young man on his offer – yes, he would like to see what went on behind those doors. He admitted to being curious about the Brethren and their daft ideas. But right now, he would be glad to get home, out of the rain.

Bobbie Rippon stirred uneasily and woke. Her clothes felt uncomfortable and the bright electric light hurt her eyes. She sat up and put her feet on the floor, shivering. The central heating had gone off hours ago and she was cold and cramped except for the warm side of her which had been next to the bed. She pushed her shoes off and fumbled, stiff-fingered, with the zip on her skirt. Her bedside clock said ten to three.

2 Tuesday

Sylvia Rippon stared across the breakfast table at her daughter. 'You look a mess,' she said. Bobbie stirred her tea and made no reply.

'Is that the only skirt you've got? It looks as if it's been slept in.'

'It has,' said Bobbie.

'What do you mean, "it has"?'

'I went to sleep in it. Last night.'

Sylvia lit a cigarette and waved the match out irritably. Bobbie knew that it annoyed her mother to discuss past events. She hated explanations. She wanted to start with a clean slate, every time. But Bobbie could not feel indignant this morning. Her eyes were still swollen and prickly, and she ached all over – particularly in the shoulder blades. She was very tired.

'Why are you up?' she asked her mother, without much interest. Sylvia tried to be bright.

'Aren't I usually up?'

'No. Not before I go.'

'Well, somebody's got to cope,' said Sylvia heroically, 'and since I'm the only parent you've got this morning, I thought I'd better do my motherly duty.'

'Where's Dad?'

Sylvia shrugged. 'You know what he's like. One breath of criticism and he just....' She spread her hands helplessly. 'He's so *insecure*, you see. Men are so *childish*.'

Bobbie did not want to hear her mother's views about men this morning. 'Where did he go?'

'How should *I* know? I'd be the last person he'd tell – not

61

that I believe what he tells me anyway. Last time he went flaring off he said he'd driven down to Brighton. Brighton! I ask you!'

Sylvia suddenly looked suspicious. 'Here, he didn't tell *you* about it, did he?'

'No.' Bobbie's small, pointed face had a closed-up, neutral look which Sylvia found momentarily alarming. She frowned.

'Are you all right, darling?'

Bobbie nodded. Her lips quivered and she ducked her head to avoid her mother's gaze. When she looked up, her face was composed into its blank mask again. 'Yes, thanks,' she said.

'But, sweetie, is that the only skirt you've got?'

'It's my only school skirt.'

'Well, look' – Sylvia opened her bag and took out a five pound note – 'buy yourself a new one after school. And you can get yourself something nice with the change. There!' She smiled radiantly, feeling like a cross between Britannia and Mother Earth, all flowing draperies and smooth, round, maternal arms.

'Thanks,' said Bobbie mechanically, continuing to stir her tea.

'Oh, charming!' flared Sylvia. 'Nice to be appreciated! It's a damned sight more than your worthless father ever did for you, my girl!'

'Better be going,' muttered Bobbie. She escaped from the table, took her blazer out of the cupboard and put it on. 'Have you seen my hat? I'm supposed to show it to Mrs Newley.'

'*Hat?* Good God, you know I'm sick with worry about your father and you bother me about a hat? Don't you realise he may be *dead*? I suppose you'd like that, wouldn't you – you'd like to see me going out to work, slaving away to support you, having no one else to love except you – that's what you want, isn't it? Everything centred round *you*. God, you selfish little bitch!'

Bobbie opened the front door. 'Goodbye,' she said, and went out, shutting it hard behind her. She could still hear her mother's voice as she walked down the path, but she couldn't hear the words.

David Rippon had left Brighton too late to miss the morning traffic. He cursed himself for coming east of Croydon to use his normal route up to town. Why hadn't he gone straight up until he met the Kingston bypass and then taken Richmond Bridge and Westway? Bloody Camberwell was jammed stiff this morning.

He eased the Jaguar round the Oval and up the traffic-choked one-way system south of Vauxhall, his bumper almost touching that of the car in front. Suddenly he found an unexpectedly empty lane. He shot down the straight stretch then braked decisively for the turn, swinging wide to be in the left-hand lane at the lights. They were green. David skimmed narrowly past the front of an elderly Morris Minor, grinning at the terrified expression on the face of the woman driver as she braked hard to let him pass. He rammed his foot hard on the accelerator to make a fast left-hand sweep on to Vauxhall Bridge then, swearing, trod furiously on his brakes. A trade van, leaving it late, had filtered out into the bridge lane in front of him. There was no room to stop. The front bumper caught the van two-thirds of the way along its side, just in front of the rear wheel. There was a screech of metal as David wrenched the car away, tearing out a section of the van's panelling and then, in a moment of horror, he was aware of a loud horn blaring in his ears as the petrol tanker on his left loomed over him.

The woman driving the Morris Minor watched in astonishment as the Jaguar, trapped between the tanker and the van, seemed to unfold like a metal blossom; bonnet cover, hub caps, bumpers and wings exploded upwards in weirdly graceful parabolas. From the shut-windowed seclusion of the Morris, the clanging, screeching, tearing sound of ripped and hammered metal did not reach her. It all seemed to happen in slow, half-comic pantomime.

A traffic jam rapidly built up all the way back to Camberwell Green as access to the bridge was totally blocked by the wrecked Jaguar and van, and the badly damaged tanker. For this reason it took the ambulance a long time to reach David despite its flashing light and the deafening urgency of its siren.

Fanny knocked at the staff room door, and waited. It was opened by Mary Ross, fulfilling her duty as a junior staff member.

'Can I speak to Miss Perkins, please?'

Mary glanced over her shoulder, past the screen which prevented any girl in the corridor from seeing into the private recesses of the staff room. Miss Perkins was relaxing in an armchair, drinking her first cup of tea of the day.

'Er – she seems to be busy,' said Mary. 'Can I give her a message?'

'She's got my play script,' said Fanny. 'And I *must* have it back. It's important.'

'Oh, I see,' said Mary, looking worried. 'Just a minute.'

Leaving the door ajar, she went across to Miss Perkins. 'I'm awfully sorry to bother you,' she said, 'but Fanny Anthony's at the door. She says—'

'Ah, yes!' To Mary's surprise, Miss Perkins got briskly to her feet. 'I want to see that girl.' She bustled across to the door, pausing on the way to pick up a bulky sheaf of duplicated papers from the table.

'Now!' she greeted Fanny, 'what have you to say for yourself?'

Fanny's face assumed the wooden expression she habitually wore when spoken to by teachers she regarded as hostile. 'Sorry I was reading in your lesson, Miss Perkins,' she said mechanically.

'I should think so. Not only is it rude, but it implies conceit. You are not so perfect as to need no further instruction, Fanny.'

'No, Miss Perkins.'

'Here is your script. And when, may I ask, is this master-piece to be performed?'

'We open in three weeks' time, on the twenty-ninth. It runs for seven days, Saturday to Saturday, no performance on Sunday.'

Miss Perkins nodded, secretly amused by the fluency of the pat answer. 'It sounds a very big undertaking – what about your homework?'

'It's half-term week,' said Fanny coldly.

'So it is.' Miss Perkins permitted herself a fleeting smile. 'Right, off you go – and no more reading in my lessons!'

'No, Miss Perkins. Thank you, Miss Perkins.' Fanny did not smile back.

Miss Perkins closed the door. 'That girl,' she remarked generally, 'is a sulker.'

'You can say that again,' said Mrs Newley.

'I only hope she has the talent to justify the sulks,' continued Miss Perkins. 'I read the script of this play she's in. It's very modern.' Iris Newley gave a confident shudder of sympathy. 'But it's not to be taken lightly,' Miss Perkins went on smoothly. 'Not by any means. We must not be old-fashioned and there is more to drama than Shaw and Shakespeare, isn't there?'

'Oh – quite,' said Mrs Newley. And when Miss Perkins had gone back to her armchair, Iris raised her eyes to the ceiling, much to the amusement of some of the other teachers.

The girls of Four N were packing their books for the morning's lessons and exchanging all the news and gossip which had accumulated since four o'clock on the previous evening.

Iris Newley totalled her register, closed it and slid it into her top drawer. She stared round at the chattering girls without enthusiasm and then stiffened slightly as she caught sight of Bobbie Rippon's mop of unruly hair. Hats, she thought. She beckoned to Fanny and Bobbie.

'You two, didn't I tell you to see me this morning, first thing?'

They exchanged exaggeratedly puzzled stares.

'Oh, come on.' Iris was in no mood for feigned innocence.

'You know damn well I said show me your hats this morning. Now, where are they?'

'I forgot,' said Fanny.

'I can't find mine,' said Bobbie. 'I did ask Mum but she said she hasn't seen it.'

The Battle of the Hats had been raging in the school for years but had lately entered a more angry phase. Miss Beacon was adamant that the school uniform should include the school hat, and insisted that the staff must present a united front in enforcing the wearing of hats at all times when the girls were seen outside the building in their uniforms. The current fourth year had, however, come very near to an open refusal to comply with this rule. The more militant among them incurred so many detentions that a member of staff intent upon imposing punishment was forced into the humiliating position of 'booking' the next available detention-free day, sometimes two or three weeks ahead. The whole business, Mrs Newley reflected, was a stupid waste of time because they were battling on a losing wicket. She looked at the two girls standing in front of her. They were clearly totally unrepentant.

Bobbie, staring back, allowed her eyes to unfocus so that Mrs Newley's red jersey slid outwards at the edges to a meaningless blur. Her eyes still felt sore from last night's weeping and she was suddenly aware that she would very much like to go back to bed. A yawn gathered in her throat, stretched outwards and crackled in her ears. Covertly, she took a deep breath to try and subdue it.

'Roberta!' shouted Mrs Newley, her face almost as red as her jersey, 'How *dare* you yawn in my face when I'm speaking to you! I will not stand for this damned impertinence! You break school rules which *I* have to make you keep, whether I like it or not, and then you do a blasted insolent thing like that! All right, if that's the way you want it you'd better go and tell Miss *Beacon* where your hat is. And if *she* can understand a household where a thing as big as a school hat can be lost, it's more than I can.'

Bobbie's lips tightened but she remained silent.

'Oh, don't stand there looking like a – a bloody *goat*,' said Mrs Newley, striking an apt comparison for the impassive-eyed girl, 'just go and sit down. And for God's sake bring your hats tomorrow.'

As Bobbie and Fanny returned to their desks, some girls grinned and some looked prim, some nodded their support while others touched their hair and looked about them absently. Subtly but unmistakably, 4N smiled its smile of triumph. Another round in the battle had been won.

As they climbed the stairs which led to the biology lab on the first floor, Bobbie said, 'do you think she *will* report me to Miss Beacon?'

'No!' scoffed Fanny. 'Not her. She's just pretending, or she wouldn't have said bring your hats tomorrow. It's all pretend. The staff pretend they believe in what they're doing and we pretend to respect them and our parents pretend they're thinking of our futures when really all they're thinking is, I have to work so why the hell shouldn't they? One of these days we'll all stop pretending and then everything will fall apart and we can think of something better.'

Bobbie was not listening. Grey stockings, women prisoners wore, made of cotton, wrinkled at the ankles; shapeless cardigans and broad-striped dresses of harsh calico ... she dragged her mind back to the present with a little shiver.

'Oh, well,' she said. 'She can't kill me, I suppose.'

'That's the spirit,' said Fanny.

'I went for a walk last night,' said Colin, busy tidying up the Puffins' shelf.

'M'm?' Helen was sorting through a handful of invoices. The paper work was much the most demanding part of running a bookshop.

'I got stopped by a policeman.'

Helen looked up. 'Why?'

'No reason. He seemed to think that law-abiding citizens didn't go for walks. I just thought I'd tell you because I had to give my place of work. Among other things.'

Helen put down the invoices. 'But, Colin, that's disgraceful,' she said. 'You were stopped and questioned, just like that, for nothing? Where were you?'

'Down past the school on that unmade road. I was looking at a frog.'

'Oh, they're a bit sensitive about that road. It's not very well lit, you know, and girls have been attacked there from time to time.'

'I see.' Colin laughed rather bitterly. 'Well, that puts a new light on it. I thought I was just a potential burglar but it seems that I was really a sex maniac in disguise.'

'If they come here,' said Helen, 'I shall assure them that you have never once attempted to ravage me behind the Ladybirds. Or anywhere else.'

'Thanks,' said Colin. 'I'm sure that's all they'll need. But look – if my mother should happen to come in – I mean, she does sometimes – well, you won't mention anything about it, will you? It's my dad, you see. He'd be horrified to think any of the family had anything to do with the police.'

'Colin, of *course* I won't! I wouldn't dream of it. But you mustn't worry, you know. This kind of thing happens to lots of people. I mean, Stewart was stopped once when he was out very late on a case. They wanted to see his licence and all that sort of thing. It doesn't *mean* anything.'

'It doesn't mean anything to *you*,' corrected Colin. 'But then, you're a lady.'

'A woman.'

'A lady. You'd say, "Good evening, constable," in your pleasant Cambridge voice and he'd shuffle off, tugging at his greasy forelock as he went.'

'Oh, honestly Colin, you're absolutely obsessed with the social strata! Do you realise, you're a most frightful snob?'

'*Me?*'

'Yes, you! An inverted snob, like someone looking at the world upside down, with his head between his knees.'

'Huh!' said Colin darkly, 'it's all very well for *you*.' He patted a row of C. S. Lewis into a straight frontage, and felt deeply misunderstood.

Mrs Mallalieu moved her massive bulk to the front door and opened it to admit Mr Dovedale, builder and decorator. 'Come along in,' she said, and gave a wheezy cough. 'Oh, do excuse me.' She patted her lips with a tiny hanky.

'Chesty weather,' said Mr Dovedale. Following Mrs Mallalieu up the stairs, he noticed the portrait which Mary found so hauntingly repulsive. 'Hand done?' he inquired, indicating it with a horny thumb.

'My first effort!' beamed Mrs Mallalieu.

She elaborated on the subject of her art class, her art teacher and her art materials all the way up the two flights of stairs and across the landing to the bathroom door. 'Are you – fond – of pictures?' she asked breathlessly, her hand on the knob.

'No,' said Mr Dovedale. 'Painting all day, aren't I? You want a rest from it, nights.'

'Everyone,' said Mrs Mallalieu, 'to their tastes.' And she opened the bathroom door.

Mr Dovedale stared in. 'Christ,' he said.

The school secretary tapped on the classroom door and put her head in. 'Sorry to interrupt,' she said, 'but have you got 4N with you?'

'Yes, I have,' said Miss Evans, chalk poised.

'Miss Beacon would like to see Roberta Rippon, please. Right away.'

A ripple of excitement ran through the class. Bobbie! In big trouble about her hat!

Bobbie stared at Fanny, stricken. So Mrs Newley *had* reported her! Fanny put up her hand. 'Shouldn't I go, too?' she said boldly. 'I forgot my hat as well.'

The secretary looked very uncomfortable. 'No, just Roberta,' she insisted.

'Run along, Roberta.' Miss Evans hated interruptions.

'Good luck!' hissed Fanny.

Bobbie walked down the stairs with the secretary, who seemed, she thought, to be behaving rather oddly, giving her little smiles as if she was a small child going to the dentist. The secretary tapped on Miss Beacon's door, listened with head bent for the ping of her admission bell, then ushered Bobbie inside, closing the door behind her.

'Roberta. Come in and sit down.' Miss Beacon took off her glasses and held them in both hands, her arms resting on the leather-edged blotter. She looked concerned rather than cross. Bobbie stared at her as she sat down in the high-backed, wide-seated chair. Was she going to be expelled? Unfit to be in this school?

'Now, Roberta. I have something to tell you, dear, which is rather grave but not as bad as it might be, so I don't want you to leap to any alarming conclusions.'

Bobbie's mind began to race. Not the hat, then. But what? *What?*

'I'm afraid your father was involved in a road accident this morning. He—'

'Is he dead?' The question had to be asked.

'No, Roberta, he's not. I do assure you of that. I rang the hospital myself and they say he is reasonably comfortable. Your mother is very upset, of course.'

Bobbie nodded, trying to think. Daddy. No. She must not let her mind go lurching off that way, or she would cry and cry, and she needed to be sensible now because Mum would be in a terrible state.

'I'd better go home,' she said.

Miss Beacon studied the girl carefully. There was something very strange about her lack of reaction. After the first shocked flush of colour to her face, she had closed down a kind of defence mechanism and now looked as tense and wary, sitting in the big, leather-seated chair with her hands pressed together, as if she was on trial.

'Your mother is going to the hospital this afternoon to see your father,' Miss Beacon told her. 'And she would like you to

70

go with her. Now, Roberta, my dear, it can be a distressing experience to see someone very soon after an accident and I did ask your mother to think about it carefully. The hospital tells me that your father is under sedation at present, so there is no possibility that he will be able to talk to you. If your mother changes her mind, you can come back here, you know, and someone will be with you. But of course, the decision is up to your mother.'

Bobbie found herself in a state of dreamlike calm. Miss Beacon looked so anxious that it was almost funny. Mum had given her a nasty shock, you could see that. The Outside World had come pushing its way into her nice, safe school. Oh, but how nice it was, really. And how safe. Bobbie sighed. 'I'd better go,' she said.

Miss Beacon nodded. Then she banged the bell push on her desk and sat back in her chair until the secretary came in.

'Mrs Williams,' she said, 'Roberta is going home. Will you make sure that Mrs Newley knows?'

'Yes, of course.' The secretary gave Bobbie another sympathetic smile and went out again.

'What about getting home?' asked Miss Beacon. 'You live some distance away, don't you – I'll ask one of the staff to give you a lift.'

'Oh no, it's all right,' said Bobbie, embarrassed by the idea. 'I can get the bus. And I want to tell my friend first, so she can look after my books and things.'

'Are you sure, dear?'

'Yes, really. Thank you very much, though.'

Miss Beacon came round her desk and stood before Bobbie. 'My dear,' she said, 'you will need a great deal of fortitude in the next few days. If I can help you in any way at all, feel free to come and ask me. Now, do remember that.'

'Yes. Thank you. I will.'

'God be with you.' Miss Beacon put her hand on the girl's shoulder for a moment and Bobbie found that the atmosphere was suddenly highly charged with emotion. She turned abruptly and left the room, closing the door behind her very quietly. Miss Beacon's kindness was somehow extremely upsetting.

Morning break had just begun and the corridors were crowded with girls. Bobbie, attempting to return from Miss Beacon's study to the first floor classroom, was met head-on by a tide of girls cascading down the stairs, heading for the chilly fresh air of the tarmac yard.

'Bobbie!' yelled Fanny from halfway up the stairs, 'I've got your basket!'

Bobbie waved acknowledgement.

'Did you get in a row?' asked Rosie Mowlem.

'Was it about your hat?'

'What did she say?'

They clustered round, bright with curiosity. Bobbie shrugged. 'Oh, nothing much.' She could not possibly tell them about her father. Not all at once. Not here. Oh, *where* was Fanny?

Bobbie cast a desperate glance up the stairs. Fanny, who had almost reached her, interpreted it correctly and took instant action. 'Sandie,' she said, 'bung these in the classroom for us, there's a dear!' Sandie opened her mouth to protest but, on catching a massive wink from Fanny, obligingly took on Bobbie's straw basket and Fanny's cardboard box and staggered off, laden like a pack-horse.

'You all right?' asked Fanny. 'You look a bit odd.'

'Don't know,' said Bobbie. She was beginning to feel slightly sick.

Fanny pushed open the swing door which led to the gym changing room. 'In,' she said, guiding Bobbie before her. 'Now, sit down there.'

Bobbie sat down on a bench. A cotton plimsoll bag dangling from a hook bumped against her left ear. 'Dad's had an accident,' she said. 'Mum rang up.'

'An accident? What sort of accident?'

'A road accident. He's in hospital.'

'Oh, Lord. I bet your mother's in a state.'

Bobbie nodded. 'I said I'd go home. I mean, I'll have to, really.'

'What a pity your mother doesn't drive,' said Fanny practically.

'Yes. But Dad's got the car anyway. I mean—' and suddenly Bobbie saw in her mind's eye tangled metal and smashed windows, oil and petrol and blood. The horror grew and grew, and this time she could not pull her mind away from it.

'You all right, love?' asked Fanny. 'You look a bit funny.'

'Feel sick.' Bobbie's face was chalk-white.

'Put your head down. Right down between your knees.' Fanny put her hand between her friend's shoulders and held her down firmly. After some time she felt Bobbie stiffen a little, resisting her. She helped her to sit up. 'Are you all right?'

'M'm.'

'Look, you ought to go up to the medical room and lie down. It's the shock, you see. It's not your *fault* or anything. It would happen to anyone.'

'Must go home.' Bobbie shivered. 'Isn't it cold in here.'

Fanny saw the sleeve of a sweater sticking out of the PE bag just above her head. She hauled it out and made Bobbie put it on. 'There,' she said. 'That's better. Now look, are you really going home?'

'I must, Fanny. Really. You don't know Mum.'

Fanny grinned. 'Oh, yes, I do! Remember that time when the goldfish had died and she couldn't touch it? I put it down the loo and she said I was a hard little bitch.'

Bobbie managed a watery smile.

'Come on,' said Fanny. 'We'll go and get your coat. Anything else you need? Purse or anything?'

'In my skirt pocket,' said Bobbie. 'There's biology homework—'

'Oh, don't be silly. They can whistle for that.'

Fanny escorted her friend out of the changing room and down the stairs to Cloakroom D and stuffed her unresistingly into her coat. Then she put on her own.

'What are you doing?' asked Bobbie.

'Taking you home, of course,' said Fanny firmly. 'At least as far as the bus stop, anyway.'

'You'll get into awful trouble.'

'No, I won't. I'm doing a Good Deed. And anyway, trouble is better than boredom.'

Another rumble of feet sounded overhead, announcing the end of morning break and as the two girls left the building they were watched by some hundreds of curious spectators, from dozens of different windows.

'What a long wait,' said Bobbie, after what seemed like hours at the bus stop. 'It would have been quicker to walk.'

'Yes, but it might *not* have been quicker,' argued Fanny. 'I mean, if a bus had come when we were first here, you'd have been home by now.'

'Yes, but I'm not. Oh, Fanny, I do hope you won't get into too much trouble. You ought to go back. I'm all right now, really I am.'

'What, and leave my best friend reeling with shock? No, I'll stay till the bus comes. At least I'll have missed Latin.'

'Here it is! Thanks for coming, Fanny.'

'Ring me up tonight, yes? Don't forget!'

'OK.' Bobbie got on to the bus and its sliding doors hissed shut. She turned to wave and Fanny realised that Bobbie was still wearing the jersey she had pulled out of the bag in the changing room. She could sort that out later, she thought. She waved energetically as the bus pulled away and then, with great reluctance, turned to walk back to school.

Mary Ross walked into Room 22 and put her case down on the desk. The girls of 4 N were sprawled in their desks, gossiping excitedly. They took no notice of Mary's presence. There was, she noticed, no sign of the two 'ringleaders' as Miss Perkins had called them.

'Good morning!' she said loudly. Eyebrows were raised and one or two of the girls less centrally involved in the conversation turned round to face the front. The volume of the gabble dropped fractionally, then rose again.

'Will you please be quiet!' shouted Mary. 'And you – what's your name?'

'Clara Bloggs.'

'Clara, will you please shut the door.'

There was a shout of laughter. 'That's not Clara Bloggs!' someone bawled, 'that's Queen Victoria!'

Fooled again. Mary should have known. Cursing herself, she cast a nervous glance at the door, expecting the solid figure of Miss Perkins to appear at any moment.

'Will you please all sit down,' she said firmly. 'And you, whatever your name is, please shut the door.'

The girl grinned and gave the door an insultingly half-hearted poke with her foot. It swung a little way but did not shut and she turned to sit down.

'Oh, no, you don't!' Mary suddenly flared with anger. 'Come here!'

Still grinning, the girl approached. Mary felt a wild desire to hit her. She was so angry that she forgot to worry about discipline or Miss Perkins or anything else. She stared at the girl as she controlled her fury, dispassionately observing the rather top-heavy white blouse and over-obvious green eye-shadow, put on deliberately, Mary suspected, as a sign of contempt for the new teacher's authority. Under Mary's scrutiny the girl glanced away. Mary pressed her momentary advantage.

'Look,' she said, 'when I ask you your name it is simply so that I can call you by your proper name instead of saying, "hey, you!" which I think is rude. Don't you?'

The girl shrugged again, but this time the gesture was faintly apologetic.

'What *is* your name?' pursued Mary.

'Mary Coppard.'

'My name is Mary, too. Mary Ross. I'm sorry to say something as personal as this, but I'm afraid your eye-shadow isn't very successful. It makes your eyes look smaller rather than larger and that's not really the idea, is it? So try and do a little better or else leave it off altogether. Now, if you'll shut the door we can get on.'

Mary spoke crisply, still buoyed up by her anger. Mary Coppard shut the door then sat down, her round face slightly pink.

'Hey,' said Sandie McIver, 'd'you know you're the first teacher who's told us her Christian name?'

'Perhaps I'm the only one who's *got* a Christian name,' suggested Mary, raising a general smile.

'D'you know anyone else's name?' Sandie pursued. 'What's Miss Perkins called?'

'I honestly don't know. I don't even know your name. You come from Scotland, though, don't you?'

'Yes, from Dundee. Sandie McIver.'

'My grandfather lives in Aberdeen,' said Mary. But nobody was interested and a mutter of conversation had begun again. Mary had the impression that it was more than mere chatter which absorbed them so much and, as if confirming this, Rosie Mowlem suddenly stood up with something of the air of a spokesman. As she did so, a rustly silence fell.

'Miss Ross,' said Rosie, 'can we ask you something?'

'Yes, of course.'

'Is it true that Bobbie's been expelled? And Fanny?'

'Expelled?' Mary was shocked. 'Whatever for?'

'For not wearing hats.'

'Oh, of course not,' said Mary. 'You couldn't be expelled for anything as silly as that.'

'But they've gone home, both of them!' said Sandie. 'We saw them!'

'And Bobbie had to go and see Miss Beacon,' said someone else. A bedlam of talk had broken out again.

'Oh, do be *quiet*!' said Mary desperately, 'I can't hear myself *think*. Look, this going home business might be about anything. Trouble at home or – or illness or—' She ran out of ideas.

'Or expulsion,' said Mary Coppard darkly.

'Well, there's no point in wasting time in speculation when none of us actually knows anything,' said Mary. 'But I'll find out at lunch time and if you're still in the dark you can come to the staff room door and ask me. Now, about this Milton.'

There was a general groan.

'It's *boring*,' said Sandie.

'Not all of it,' said Mary. 'And he uses marvellous words. Great long decorative ones.'

'But people don't talk like that,' objected someone.

'You can't chuck out all the past just because it doesn't fit with the present style,' argued Mary. 'I mean, what about music? We still listen to Beethoven—'

'That's different!'

'You can have Bach and jazz and pops—' Mary was not making herself heard in the wrangling, incoherent cross-fire of opinions.

'Do shut *up*!' she yelled. They looked at her, surprised, and she went on quickly, 'it doesn't get you anywhere, all this bedlam. I don't mind talking, but for goodness' sake let's talk so that we can hear each other. All right, so Milton is boring. But there's lots of poets besides Milton.'

'They're *all* boring,' said someone, amid general laughter.

'All about the same old things. Some drippy girl—'

'Or glorious battle—'

'Or wandering lonely as a bloody cloud.'

'Hate Wordsworth.'

'Tennyson's worse. Ugh!'

'Don't you know any modern poetry?' asked Mary.

'Leonard Cohen.'

'Sexy!'

'It's all so muddled, though. You don't know what they're on about half the time.'

'Oh, nonsense,' said Mary. 'Some of it is beautifully clear. Look at people like Carl Sandburg and William Carlos Williams. It's as simple as a shopping list.'

'Never heard of them.'

'Don't you know the one about eating the plums in the ice box?' Mary persisted.

'No.'

'Then I'll say it to you. Be quiet a minute, and listen. It's called "This is Just to Say" and it's a sort of note left on the kitchen table. It goes—

' "I have eaten
the plums
that were in
the ice box

and which
you were probably
saving
for breakfast

Forgive me
they were delicious
so sweet
and so cold" '

There was a pause and then Sandie asked, 'Is that all?'
'Yes,' said Mary.
Hubbub broke out. 'That's not a poem.' 'Yes, it is, it's nice.' 'Stupid.' 'Funny sort of man he must be.' 'Read it again, Miss.' 'She didn't read it, she just *said* it.'
In the middle of the noise, the door opened and Fanny came in. There was instant silence.
'I'm sorry I'm late,' said Fanny. 'I had to go somewhere.' She made for her seat.
'Just a minute,' said Mary. 'I want to know a bit more than that. Where did you have to go?'
'I had to go somewhere with Bobbie.' Fanny was guarded, aware of the hissed questions from all over the room. 'What's happened?' 4N wanted to know. 'Where's Bobbie?'
'Fanny,' said Mary, 'I don't want you to betray any confidences but we are all very anxious about Bobbie and you seem to be the only person who knows what's going on. I'd be very glad if you'd set our minds at rest.'
Fanny looked at Mary, then nodded. 'Yes, I will,' she said.

'You see, her father's had a car accident. I thought Miss Beacon wanted to see her because she wasn't wearing a hat, but it was to tell her about the accident. She had to go home, to go to the hospital with her mother, so I took her to the bus stop. Honestly, I had to, Miss Ross. She went all faint when she was telling me about it and I wasn't sure she'd be all right.'

'Of course you had to,' said Mary. 'I'm glad you did. Is her father badly hurt, do you know?'

'I'm not sure,' said Fanny. 'Bobbie said something about concussion?'

'Well, let's hope it's not too serious,' said Mary. 'Thank you anyway, Fanny.'

When Fanny had sat down, Rosie Mowlem said, 'Miss Ross, will you say that poem for us again? Because Fanny missed it.'

'Yes,' agreed several voices, 'say it again.' One or two faces were screwed up in disagreement but there was no real opposition and, as Mary recited the poem for the second time she found that 4N were listening attentively.

Bobbie got off the bus at the corner of Orchard Walk and set out to walk the last few hundred metres to her house.

Orchard Walk, despite its name, was almost completely treeless. Somewhere under the pavements, reflected Bobbie, lay the dead roots of the orchard which must once have grown here. White and dead in the dead earth, cemented over like a tomb. Her father would be like that, rotting under the earth, if he died. Bobbie gave a panic-stricken gasp which was almost a sob, and broke into a run, frightened by the sudden nightmare. She came to the cul-de-sac which led to three modern, architect-designed houses, one of which belonged to her parents. Here the trees had been replaced. Silver birches grew in carefully sited groups on the casual lawns between the glass and timber houses. Paving stones let into the grass formed a path to each front door and a driveway to each garage. The cul-de-sac was called Fonteyn Court and was ironically referred to by the occupants of Orchard Walk as Beverley Hills.

Bobbie trotted round the side of the house to the kitchen

door which was her normal way in. It was bolted. She shook it by its spun aluminium handle, then rapped on it with her knuckles. 'Mum!' she shouted.

There was no answer. Bobbie called again, with increasing anxiety, then retraced her steps to the front door, digging in her purse for her key. She let herself in and banged the door behind her, loudly. 'Mum?'

The house was perfectly quiet. Listening intently, Bobbie could hear the hum of the deep freeze in the kitchen. Nothing else. She ran upstairs and looked in her mother's pink-carpeted bedroom. There was as usual a clutter of make-up bottles, clothes on the backs of chairs, discarded tights on the floor. None of this was unusual. Sylvia despised tidiness. 'So *bourgeois*,' she would say.

Bobbie looked in every room in the house then went into the kitchen and perched uneasily on a black leather bar stool. Her mother had gone out. But why? Why should she ring up the school to ask Bobbie to come home, and then not be here?

The thought came to Bobbie that the hospital must have rung up. 'Mrs Rippon, your husband has suffered a serious relapse. I'm afraid you must come at once if you want to see him.' She could have left a note, though.

Bobbie stared round helplessly. There was nothing she could do. She thought of her father as he used to be, when she was very small. He used to smell so lovely, a big, rich mixture of tobacco and earth because he used to do the garden himself then, before he was so busy and went away so often at the weekends. It was because of management conferences, he said.

She gazed at the kitchen, at its stainless steel tiles which reflected back distorted, sectionalised images of herself, at the row of pine veneered cupboards where the food mixer and the coffee grinder and the electric bread knife were hidden. Bobbie knew there was no food in the cupboards except for several half-finished packets of cornflakes, all soft, and a very large number of jars of pickles and jams which had been opened and partly eaten. There were at least three packets of slightly stale cheese crackers, a tube of chocolate spread and a tin of instant coffee.

Bobbie got down from her stool and began to stack some of the dirty dishes into the washing-up machine. The activity soothed her anxieties and she managed to concentrate fully on the sticky, brown-stained mugs and the crumb-scattered plates, several of which had stubbed-out cigarettes on them. She switched on the refuse disposal unit and swilled water round the sink until the pile of crusts and eggshells which had been left there had disappeared. She wiped the stainless steel surfaces, threw the damp cloth into the disused washing-up bowl in the cupboard under the sink and shut the door. There. Everything hidden. Everything neat.

Perhaps, thought Bobbie, she should have something to eat. The brass ship's clock on the wall said twelve-forty. At school 4N would be in the dining hall since they were on first sitting. Bobbie opened the fridge. There were three pints of milk in the door rack, all of which were without their cream as Sylvia always took it to put in her coffee. There was nothing in the least bit appealing and the smell of something mouldy made Bobbie wrinkle her nose. She shut the fridge door, then took a slice of bread out of the packet in the bread bin, spread it with margarine and pickle and topped it with a hunk of cheese. It did not take long to eat although she nibbled at it without appetite. She drank some milk from one of the bottles then put it back in the fridge. She put her knife in the washing-up machine. Then there was nothing else to do.

Where was her mother? Depression swept over Bobbie in a black tide. The silent kitchen seemed oppressive and timeless, as sealed away from the outside world as a space capsule. It enclosed Bobbie with its black and silver surfaces, a mocking, unfunctioning machine only minimally used by its owners, who were always busy doing something else. But what do we do that is so important? Bobbie wondered. What do we *want*? Mum – irritable, frustrated, flicking angry cigarette ash, drooping those heavy eyelids as if everything was agonisingly boring. And Dad, hardly speaking, looking neutrally at nobody, locked away in a different life which he would not or could not share. And me.

Bobbie pushed her fingers through her mop of frizzy hair. Her hands were sticky. Impulsively, she decided to have a bath. It was a relief to have settled on a course of action. She went upstairs to her room, pulling off her school tie on the way. She took off her white blouse and her navy skirt and left them on the floor where they fell, kicked off her shoes and then sat down on her bed and peeled off her white socks. Then she took off her bra and pants and stretched luxuriously, enjoying the sensation of air on her skin. With her father in hospital, she thought guiltily, she ought not to take pleasure in such trivial things. She ought to think and feel in a bigger sort of way, somehow, in a manner more suited to the dark uncertainty of life. But how? She went into the carpeted bathroom and turned on the hot tap. In the mirror tiles, as in the kitchen, a thousand fragmented Bobbies shifted and flickered, no single one of them reflecting a true image.

Fanny sat in the corner of Cloakroom D with Sandie McIver, well screened from view by a forest of navy-blue macs. The place smelt muddy and faintly rubbery, but it was better than being outside, where a thin, cold rain blew mistily across the tarmac but failed to qualify as a 'wet break'. Fanny was not keen on going outside, even at the best of break times, to walk in long strings of arm-in-arm girls round and round the playground. And Sandie McIver, with her characteristic seriousness, had something to ask.

'Hey, Fanny – d'you think Bobbie's all right? Her mother's a bit weird, you know. My brother saw her the other night and he said she was – well – very odd.'

Fanny frowned. 'When did he see her?'

'Oh, he bumped into Bobbie on the footbridge – I mean, quite literally. You know what Colin's like, he goes off into dreams and doesn't notice where he's going. And he walked home with her. I think he's a bit gone on her, as a matter of fact.'

'Is he? Good old Bob – he's rather dishy, your bruv, if you like red hair, that is.'

'Too bad if you don't!' said Sandie, shaking her own carroty mop. 'No, but Fanny, listen. You mustn't tell anyone you know about this, or try to *do* anything – promise?'

'Don't be daft, Sandie, how can I promise until I know what it is?'

Sandie pursed her lips judiciously. 'Then I'd better not tell you,' she said. 'I'm sorry. I shouldn't have said.'

Fanny was furious. 'Oh *Sandie*!' she said, thumping her fist on the wooden bench on which they sat. 'That's not fair.'

'Yes, it is. Colin said I wasn't to tell anyone and I won't.'

'Yes, you will, you'll tell me. Whatever it is, I'll be silent as the grave.'

'And you won't *do* anything?'

'And I won't – oh, come *on*, Sandie!'

'Well, all right, then. Colin said Bobbie's mother was drunk. So there. He said he thinks she's the kind of person who's always drunk. And apparently Bobbie more or less admitted that it happened a lot. That's why I wondered if she was all right, going home today. Now, Fanny, you're not to go rushing round there or anything.'

Fanny was staring at her friend intently. 'Sandie, I do believe you may be right. I don't know Bobbie's mother very well – Bob comes to my house rather than me going to hers—'

'That may be why,' interrupted Sandie.

'Quite. But I have seen her mother in an awful tizzy from time to time. You know, sort of shouting and horrid. I just thought she was very bad-tempered – but I suppose she could be your actual alky. I'll ask my father about it. Being a doctor, he's bound to know a bit.'

'Fanny, you promised!'

'Oh, don't worry. I'll be ever so tactful. I'll say I was reading some article in the *Guardian* or something. He never thinks things have a personal meaning, anyway. When Matthew described all the symptoms of chicken-pox it took him ages to realise that Matthew *had* it.'

Approaching footsteps sounded loudly on the stone floor and a prefect put her head round the end of the coat rack.

'Out,' she said.

'Oh, go on, Alva,' said Fanny. 'The bell will go at any minute. Can't you turn a blind eye for once?'

'No, I can't. There's no point in having prefects' duty if we let everyone get away with breaking the rules. Come on – out! Or I'll report you to Miss Beacon.'

'Aw right, guv, I'll come quietly,' wheezed Fanny in her cab-driver's voice. Hand on an imaginary arthritic hip, she hobbled to the door. Sandie, as always, managed to look perfectly grave. Only when outside the door did she venture to observe, 'If you ask me, that Alva Johnson is considerably less than human.'

'Yerss,' gasped Fanny, still in character. 'Yer right there, guv. Cor, this fresh air'll be the death o' me, it will. Fair cripples yer kidneys.' And, with a cautious peep round the door to see that Alva Johnson had gone, she returned to the fuggy warmth of Cloakroom D.

Sylvia Rippon banged the door shut behind her. 'Bobbie!' she shouted, 'Bobbie! You there?'

In response, she heard the outward rush of bath water.

'Bobbie! You're not actually—' she rushed up the stairs, tripped slightly over the top one and stumbled in through the open bathroom door.

'My God!' She confronted her daughter furiously, 'you're not actually having a *bath*? When your father is probably *dying*?'

Bobbie's emotions froze into safety. 'I won't be long,' she said, rubbing at her hair with a corner of the bath towel which enfolded her.

Sylvia clenched her fists. 'You cold little bitch! I rang up your school *hours* ago and waited and waited to see if you'd condescend to come home and I ran out of cigarettes and at last I *had* to go and get some.'

From the Duke of Clarence, thought Bobbie. So that's where you've been. Might have known.

'I'm going to the hospital,' Sylvia went on. 'And I want you to come, Bobbie. It may be an important moment in your life.' Her eyes filled with tears. 'You are my little girl, Bobbie. My little girl. You want to see your father, don't you?'

Bobbie shook her head blindly. 'I don't know,' she said. Her mind filled with a confusion of images. Piggy-back, hand-in-hand, fizzy orangeade, up-the-stairs-to-bed. Her throat ached.

'Don't you *care?*' pursued Sylvia. 'Don't you care just one little bit?'

' 'Course I care,' muttered Bobbie. She took a deep breath. 'I'm sorry. The bus didn't come. I had to wait for ages and when I came home you weren't here. Look, go and have a cup of coffee or something. I won't be long.'

Sylvia's angry stare changed suddenly to contrition. 'Poor baby! I am sorry – oh, I really am sorry.'

'Have a cup of coffee,' repeated Bobbie with quiet desperation. Anything to get her out of the bathroom.

'Yes. Yes, I will. Cup of coffee would be nice. Thank you, darling.' Sylvia left the bathroom and found her way down to the kitchen.

'All right!' shouted Mrs Newley. 'Settle down, you lot! Register the same as this morning?'

'Bobbie's away,' said Fanny. 'Her father's had an accident.'

'Ah, yes.' Mrs Newley marked an O in the afternoon column of her register, then looked up. 'Fanny Anthony, I hear that you and Sandie were in the cloakroom at lunchtime.'

Fanny raised her eyebrows.

'What's more, when told to go out, you argued with a prefect instead of doing as you were told.'

Fanny still said nothing.

'When will you learn,' continued Mrs Newley, 'that there is nothing special about *you?* School rules apply to you the same as to everyone else. Why are you wearing brown socks?'

Fanny stretched out a leg and inspected it carefully. 'Very *dark* brown socks,' she remarked.

'*White* socks are school uniform. Or tights.'

'Brown tights.'

Mrs Newley flushed. 'Obviously tights are more or less

brown,' she snapped. 'But socks are white. And I've had quite enough of your bloody cheek. Stand *up* when I'm talking to you!'

Fanny, allowing herself to feel like Saint Sebastian being shot full of arrows, rose to her feet and gazed in a martyred fashion out of the window. Support came, totally unexpectedly, from Mary Coppard who said, 'Excuse me, Mrs Newley, but I don't think you should swear. I think it's rude.'

The class smelled blood. 'So do I', said Sandie promptly. There were nods of agreement from even the most law-abiding and timorous. Mrs Newley leaned back in her chair, the better to get them into focus as a group.

'Oh, you do, do you?' she said. 'Well, well. What a stuffy little lot we are all of a sudden. You crib at obeying a few necessary rules and yet you don't allow other people the freedom of normal colloquial expression.'

'It isn't normal in our house,' said little Annette Ives bravely.

'I don't mind swearing,' said Sandie, pursuing her argument with careful logic, 'but I don't see why there are two different standards. If we swear, we are punished. So why should you?'

'*I* don't punish you,' said Mrs Newley defensively. Fanny, still standing but free from direct attack, seized her opportunity.

'That's the whole point about school,' she said. 'We're not really thought of as people. If you want to use colloquial language then that's all right because you are a teacher and I suppose you can say you're just broad-minded.'

'Well, yes, I—'

'But we can't. I can't wear brown socks but you can wear a red jersey. We get in a row for not wearing hats, but who wears hats these days, specially hats like *that*?' There was a general shout of approval. 'If it wasn't for exams,' Fanny swept on, her face flushed with the success of her oratory, 'we could defy the school and throw out these silly rules, and there's nothing it could do because we wouldn't care if we were expelled. But we have to play ball because we *need* our O's and A's and we *need* to get to university and so we're blackmailed into behaving like puppets. We—'

'*Sit down!*' Mrs Newley's face was very red. 'Sit down at once, Fanny. How dare you!'

Fanny sat down, unhurriedly and without abandoning her challenging attitude.

'I shall report you to Miss Beacon!' said Mrs Newley. 'You needn't think you can get away with this!'

'Yes,' said Fanny, 'that's what you *have* to say, isn't it?'

For a long moment she and Mrs Newley stared at each other, each assessing the situation. Fanny, although convinced of the truth of her statement, became aware afresh of her vulnerability. Whatever would Helen say if she was expelled? Just for an instant, she was frightened. Then she reminded herself that lots of people had managed to get on the stage without having a degree, and regained her courage. She took a deep breath preliminary to continuing the argument – and at the same instant, Mrs Newley decided to opt for an armistice.

'For goodness' sake,' she said, forcing a cheerful smile, 'let's try to behave like civilised people. All right, Fanny, I won't send you to Miss Beacon this time, although most members of staff certainly would have done. There may be an element of truth in what you have said but your view of school life is ridiculously biased. And you will find as you grow up that nobody is ever free of compulsions and restrictions.'

'But—' began Fanny. Mrs Newley steam-rollered her instantly.

'Now run along, all of you. There's a class waiting to come in.'

All the way to the hospital, Bobbie tried hard to think of pleasant things. Summer holidays, hot sand under the feet, straws bobbing in a pop bottle. None of it worked very well. The train ran along an embankment, giving her a view of close-packed houses and streets which was too interesting to ignore and too boring to occupy the imagination. There was a tin bath hanging on the wall outside a kitchen; a factory yard full of thousands and thousands of empty bottles; a dog track where girls in white coats walked greyhounds, five dogs to a lead.

What would it be like in the hospital? Bobbie's concept of hospital life came from television and the cinema, since she had never been inside one herself. Her father would be very pale, his eyes closed and his head bandaged. Bobbie would take his hand and his fingers would close round hers.

Or a young doctor in a white coat would greet them, grave-faced. 'I'm afraid I have bad news for you, Mrs Rippon. Your husband died an hour ago. He talked of somebody called Bobbie.'

'She's fainted, look!' The young doctor would pick her up, lay her very gently on a couch. His face was familiar. Colin. He was like Colin. He was Colin, looking after her, grey-eyed and kind.

On Friday she was going out with Colin. That was something to hold on to. Bobbie stared out at the houses, arranged sideways to the track this time so that their perspective opened and shut like kissing gates.

Bobbie's mother was pulling on her gloves, stroking the fingers down from the tips to palms, catlike. She was a different person in public, poised and fragile, chin held up as though mink wrapped her to the ears. Her small head with its crimped, boyish hair-do, her delicate nose and heavy-lidded eyes bore witness to the habit of feeling beautiful although peevishness had long since destroyed the beauty itself. Sylvia Rippon was totally self-conscious. Her whole life was a performance. Just now she was being gracious, controlled and brave; a woman enduring suffering with magnificence.

Staring at her mother, Bobbie sighed with reluctant admiration. Her own hands, gloveless and with bitten nails, lay in her lap like two raw, pink little animals. Like young rats. The train rattled through a series of short tunnels and the pale reflection of a shock-haired girl stared dimly from the momentarily dark windows. That was Bobbie Rippon, Bobbie thought. That was what people saw. That was the outside of the machine she lived in, the body which surrounded her awareness.

The train rattled through New Cross station and started on the last long embankment before London Bridge. Bobbie leaned her head back against the prickly velour and stared at the square bulk of the Pearce Duff's custard factory which rose above the sea of roofs. This was real. The vibrating train, the stiffness of inhaled dust in the nostrils, the hands lying in the lap, the brown dirt which coated the sleepers under the rails and coated the stones between the sleepers and which was coating Bobbie's hair and lungs; the toes inside the shoes, the fag ends on the floor, all of it, all of it unbearable, jam-packed atom by atom with a kind of awful sickness. It was a nausea which crept into the most private places in Bobbie's mind and filled them with horror. This was reality. This was God's creation. This could never, never be what He had meant.

'Well, here we are,' said Sylvia. Chin well up, she opened the compartment door and got out. 'Come along.'

Bobbie stumbled out on the feet that were hers. The platform was brown. Dusty.

'Shut the door, dear.'

But a man in uniform slammed it shut before Bobbie could move, then blew piercingly on his whistle. The train moved away, gathering speed quickly.

'Can you tell me where I can find a taxi?' Sylvia asked the man.

'Up the ramp, dear, past the barrier then down the passage till you get to the road. Plenty on the rank there, outside the main line station.'

Sylvia inclined her head in thanks. 'Come along, darling,' she said. Bobbie came along.

There was a walk, then a taxi – smell of leather, lurchings from side to side as it went round corners – then the hospital door. A big place, high and modern, rather like the Festival Hall. People sitting on benches. Sylvia inquiring at the desk. Corridor. Lift.

Doors opening. Peter ward. Desmond ward. A bright young nurse with a pony tail. 'Mrs Rippon? Oh, yes. He's in there,' – pointing – 'Sister will show you.'

Sister Davis, grey-haired, short, oddly disapproving. 'Well yes, of course you can see him now you're here, but I do wish these doctors wouldn't get the relatives in right away, not unless it's critical.' She eyed Bobbie. 'Now, dear, he does look a bit untidy just now. In a day or two he'll be much better but I don't want you to expect too much of him right away.'

Entering the room, Bobbie felt breathless with dread. Tubes, a laboratory of bottles, gas cylinders. Neat white bed, the figure in it oddly dark. An arm over the bedcover with a plaster on the inside of it. A tube coming out of the plaster.

Gradually, Bobbie's extreme fright subsided a little as she stared at the motionless form under the bed clothes. Sylvia was standing at the other side of the bed, staring down at her husband's face with an expression which was difficult to define. But Bobbie did not look at her mother's face. Gathering all her courage, she leaned forward and looked instead at her father. His face was completely unfamiliar, swollen and dark, crisscrossed with abrasions and bristling with the ragged ends of black stitches. Had he been conscious, he could not have opened his eyes under the pressure of the swollen bruises. His mouth gaped insensibly, oddly babyish and fallen in, and Bobbie relised that he no longer had any front teeth. The violence of the accident was suddenly real to her.

'I think I'm going to be sick,' she said. The floor seemed to rock under her feet and Sister Davis's arm was the only solid thing in the world. Sluice room. White sink. Sick.

'Finished?' inquired Sister Davis genially. She looked much more cheerful than when Bobbie had come in with Sylvia. Bobbie nodded. She felt cold and sweaty and very ill. 'I'm sorry,' she said.

'Don't you worry a bit, my dear. Sit down here. Still feel dizzy?'

'No.'

'That's fine.' Sister Davis wiped Bobbie's face gently with a length of soft paper towel and gave her a glass of water. 'That's what I always say, people *will* come and see their nearest and dearest while they're looking a bit of a mess and of course it's a terrible shock. Much better to give it a day or two and come when they're sitting up and taking notice.'

'Will he – sit up?' Bobbie was still very frightened by the dark, sewn-up face and there was a burning sourness in the back of her throat.

'Oh, yes, you'd be surprised. He's lost a few teeth of course but look how many film stars don't have their own teeth! And the rest'll heal up as right as rain with a spot of patchwork. No, the only thing we're keeping an eye on is his tummy, just in case he's done himself any damage we don't know about yet. Now, are you all right for a minute? I'll go and get your mother.'

'Yes, I'm fine.'

Bobbie did, indeed, feel slightly better. The calm cleanness of the ward was somehow reassuring and Sister Davis inspired instant trust. How lovely it would be to stay in this warm, clean-smelling place! It was safer than outside, where things were so difficult and terrible accidents happened. Perhaps, Bobbie mused, she could be a nurse – then she would belong to this reality all the time.

Sister Davis came back with Sylvia, who advanced towards her daughter with a sympathetic smile, head on one side. 'Darling,' she said, 'are you feeling better? I didn't come rushing in – I know you experts hate anxious mothers, don't you, Sister?'

Sister Davis smiled non-committally. 'Finished with that paper towel?' she asked Bobbie.

'Yes, thank you.'

'I'll pop it in the bin, then.' As she did so, she shot Sylvia a look so filled with both contempt and wry humour that Bobbie almost smiled. Sister Davis was clearly one person whom Sylvia had failed to impress.

'The trouble with alcoholism,' said Stewart Anthony thoughtfully, 'is that it's so difficult to define. On the whole, I am inclined to think that there are two quite separate kinds of alcoholics. One is simply hooked on it in the same way as a drug addict is, but there's probably a large group for whom drinking is symptomatic of some other disturbance.'

'But can't people simply enjoy it?' objected Fanny. 'Look at you and Helen. You're always sloshing out the sherry at about six o'clock and you like wine with meals but you're not alcoholics – or are you?'

'We're potential alcoholics,' said Stewart. 'I suppose most of us are, if the truth be told. But we're pretty harmless, I think. Aren't we?'

Fanny laughed. 'Just watch it,' she said. 'If I start watering the sherry you'll know something's gone wrong.'

'I've known quite a few doctors who have become alcoholics, though,' Stewart went on. 'Starting with the six o'clock sherry when they feel pretty wound up at the end of the day and moving on to having a drink at other times when they feel tense or under strain. Alcohol isn't a stimulant, you see. People think it "bucks them up" but actually it does the opposite, calms them down. It's slightly sedative in effect. Lessens the impact of reality.'

'Is it people with nasty realities who drink, then?'

Stewart considered this. 'It's not quite as simple as that,' he said. 'Otherwise all the people who live in squalid conditions would be drunks. And they're not.'

'Can't afford it.'

'Very few alcoholics can afford it. No, I think it's people whose reality seems intolerable to *them*. I mean, there are things like boredom or frustration which don't seem important in objective terms but they can be overwhelming to the person who has to put up with them.'

'M'm. What about people like Dylan Thomas, though? He can't have been frustrated or bored, not when he was writing marvellous poetry like that.'

'But it's terribly *hard*, Fanny. I mean, getting down to writing letters is bad enough. Just think of *having* to turn out some work in order to earn some money. I don't think the life of a professional soul-searcher is an easy one. We're animals, basically. It isn't natural to us to badger our brains incessantly. We'd be much better off with a well-trained body and an understressed mind.'

'Oh *Stewart*!' said Helen, who had come in just in time to catch the last sentence, 'what a ludicrous statement! It isn't even true – I mean, athletes need terrific mental concentration. And even if it was, I don't agree. It's only through intense work that. . . .'

'I must go and do my intense homework,' said Fanny, escaping. It was all right for adults to indulge in long theoretical arguments; they had reached the leisure part of their day. She, on the other hand, had not.

'Fonteyn Court, please,' said Sylvia to the taxi driver at the station. 'The house is called Pollards. On your right as you come to it.'

'OK, lady.' The driver pushed the flag down and Bobbie sat back thankfully. It seemed far more than ten hours since she had gone to school that morning and she felt oddly light-headed. Although she had eaten nothing but some bread and cheese at lunch time and half a sausage last night she was not in the least bit hungry. Her mouth still retained a faint taste of sickness although the incident in the sluice room seemed remote now.

'Oh, isn't that nice,' said Sylvia as they approached the house. 'Marjorie's come. There's Gordon's car.'

She must have rung Marjorie this morning, thought Bobbie as she stumbled wobbly-legged from the taxi. Gathering the clan.

Marjorie opened the door. Her usually smiling face looked anxious. 'How is he?' she asked.

Sylvia nodded. 'He'll be all right,' she said, giving the impression that she had personally battled for her husband's life all day. She pulled off her gloves with fumbling fingers.

'Can I get you a drink?' asked Gordon.

Sylvia smiled up at him. 'Thank you, Gordon. What a man of the world! Just a little gin, please. And tonic.' She followed Gordon into the sitting room, leaving Bobbie with Marjorie in the hall.

'Bob, what about Dad, really?' asked Marjorie. 'Did you see him?'

Bobbie nodded. 'I thought he looked awful,' she said. 'All cut and bruised. Lots of stitches. He was unconscious but Sister Davis said he'd be much better soon. She was very nice.'

Marjorie nodded. She was standing in a temporary kind of position, one foot on the first tread of the stairs, a hand on the newel post. 'I must go and settle Keron,' she said. 'We brought his cot and he thinks it's all a great lark, going to sleep in a different house.'

'Can I come and see him?'

'Yes, of course. Don't get him all excited, though, or we'll have him up all night.'

Marjorie was exactly like Dad, thought Bobbie as she followed her sister up the stairs. Practical, basically cheerful, but impatient of 'silly' questions. Wanting things to happen efficiently and without any fuss.

Little Keron was standing up in his cot, gripping the side rail tightly in both hands, his face turned expectantly towards the door. When he saw Bobbie and his mother he began to bounce up and down excitedly, shouting and laughing.

'Hello! Aren't you getting a big boy!' said Bobbie. 'And you've got a lovely woolly rabbit! Whose is this, then?'

Keron hurled the proffered rabbit to the floor and held up his arms. 'Me up! Me up!' he shouted.

'No, you don't, young man,' said Marjorie firmly. 'Bedtime! Say bye-bye to Auntie Bobbie! – better not stay now, Bob, or he won't settle – bye-bye, Auntie Bobbie!'

Bobbie obediently went to the door, then turned and waved. 'Bye-bye, Keron!' she said. Keron's face screwed into a crumpled mask of fury and disappointment and he began to scream loudly.

'I *thought* that would happen,' said Marjorie. 'Now, do *go*, Bob, there's a dear.'

Bobbie went out of the room and stood irresolutely on the landing. She felt very bleak. If she went into her own room she would simply lie down and cry for hours, she knew. Her eyes prickled at the very thought. Her mouth was dry so she went into the bathroom and ran some water into a white tooth mug with a rose painted on it. The water tasted slightly warm and stale because she had not let the tap run but she sipped it slowly and felt her throat relax a little. She poured the rest of the water away and put the mug back in its holder. She stared at herself in the mirror, wishing as always that she could admire her reflection. Under the frizzy hair her face seemed featureless except for the little staring black eyes. It would never be a face which people would remember, Bobbie thought. Such a face could never belong to a proper, grown-up woman who would know how to talk to people and what to do.

The telephone rang and was answered downstairs. The sitting room door opened. 'Bobbie! It's for you!' shouted Gordon. 'Someone called Fanny.'

'Thank you – I'll take it upstairs,' Bobbie called back. Good old Fanny. How nice of her to ring up.

Bobbie went into her mother's room, sat on the bed and picked up the extension phone.

'Hello.' She heard the downstairs receiver replaced.

'Oh, there you are!' said Fanny. 'I rang before but I only got your brother-in-law. How's your Dad?'

'They think he'll be all right.' Tubes, black stitches – too difficult to talk about.

'Oh, good, I'm so glad. I told them at school what had happened – Miss Ross wanted to know where I'd been and she was really nice. Not cross a bit. She's all right, you know, Bob. A real person.'

'Yes.' Bobbie's eyes wandered across the objects on the dressing table. Moisturisers, fresheners, varnishes, rouges, colouring shampoos. How long did people go on keeping beautiful? Did they do it when they were old? Mascara on wrinkled eyelids, rough texture like chalking a hopscotch pitch on concrete....

'Bobbie? You still there?'

'Sorry.' Fanny's voice had slipped into the background, heard but not understood.

'Here, are you all right? Have you had meals and things?'

'Not really. We've only just got in. Mum's having a drink with Gordon. And Marjorie's putting Keron to bed. I suppose Mum rang them up.'

'How *is* your mum?'

'All right.' Why did Fanny sound so meaningful? Too much bother to ask.

'Look, Bob, you go and get something to eat and get off to bed. Don't wait for the others. I'll come round if you like.'

'No, it's OK, Fanny. Marjorie'll do something.' Bobbie was drowning in a great wave of tiredness.

'All right, if you're sure. You coming to school tomorrow?'

'Spect so.'

'See you then, then. Oh, and I must tell you about Ma Newley – it was terribly funny, Bob – we had a great set-to about swearing and. . . .'

'Tomorrow.'

'Poor old thing, you sound absolutely exhausted. Baked beans and bed, eh?'

'Yes.'

'Be seeing you then. Ciaou.'

'Bye.'

Bobbie put the phone down and slumped back against the padded headboard. In a minute, she would go down and see about supper.

Fanny frowned. She had promised Sandie that she wouldn't rush in and do anything about Bobbie and her mother – but something needed to be done. She doodled an ornamental elaboration of the drug company heading on the message pad (supplied free to doctors) and thought. Then she picked up the receiver and dialled.

'Mr McIver? Oh, it's Fanny Anthony here . . . no, it's not really Sandie I want to speak to. It's Colin.'

Colin walked up the path to the front door of Bobbie's house with some trepidation. He was not at all sure what he was going to say. As he reached the doorstep he could hear music playing loudly, and a babble of voices. For a moment he hesitated. Perhaps Fanny had exaggerated the whole thing. It didn't sound like a household that had suffered a serious accident to one of its number. But she had taken the trouble to ring up. And she had sounded quite worried. Colin rang the bell.

After a pause, the porch light above his head was switched on and he blinked in the sudden brilliance. The door was opened by neither Bobby nor her mother. It was a dark-haired, solidly-built girl who stood there. She gave him a ready smile combined with an inquiring lift of the eyebrows and said, 'Good evening – can I help you?' There was a professionalism in her manner which made Colin feel as if he had come for an interview for a job.

'My name's Colin McIver,' he said. 'I'm a friend of Bobbie's. I heard about her father's accident and I just wondered – well – if there was anything I could do.'

'That's very kind of you,' said the girl. 'Come in for a minute.'

Colin followed her into the hall where the jazzy music sounded louder than ever. The girl reached behind her to close the sitting room door. It was obvious that she had no intention of taking Colin any further into the house.

'Actually,' said the girl confidentially, 'Bobbie's fast asleep. I went up to call her for supper and found her flat out on one of the beds. She seemed much too dozy to eat anything so I just tucked her into her own bed and left her. I think it's all been a bit of a shock.'

'Ay, well, it would be,' said Colin. 'How *is* Mr Rippon?'

'I haven't seen him myself,' said the girl. 'Oh – I'm Marjorie, by the way. Bobbie's sister. The hospital seem to think there's nothing much more than concussion but I expect we'll know more tomorrow.'

'That's good,' said Colin. 'I mean, a motor accident. . . .'

'Quite,' said Marjorie. 'Can I give Bobbie any message for you?'

Colin felt himself dismissed. 'Just give her—' my love, he was going to say, but he checked himself. 'Give her my very best wishes and tell her I'll ring her tomorrow,' he said. 'At about six.' 'Love' would be all right in Scotland but this girl had a cool formality which he found unnerving.

'Six o'clock. Right, I'll make a note of that so she's sure to get the message,' said Marjorie. 'Thank you so much for calling.' She opened the door, gave Colin a final smile and ushered him out, just as Sylvia emerged from the sitting room, glass in hand.

'Marjorie darling, what *are* you doing out here?' she demanded, waving her cigarette imperiously. She seemed quite unaware of Colin's presence on the doorstep. 'Come back and join the party. Do you know that your gorgeous Gordon is a lovely dancer? Aren't you, Gordon – a *lovely* dancer?'

'Fan – tastic,' said Gordon, with a wink at his wife. 'All we need is a million metres of ice-blue tulle with hand-sewn sequins.'

Colin had retreated from the doorstep but Sylvia's laughter reached him clearly. As Marjorie shut the door he swung round and stared at it, fists clenched. What kind of people were these, who laughed and giggled while the man of the house was ill in hospital? It was no fit place for Bobbie, *that* was certain. She was so small. She didn't look strong. Somebody should be looking after her properly and seeing that she had good food and decent care. Colin stared up at the first floor windows, looking for a sign of Bobbie's presence, but there was nothing. The bedroom windows were dark and silent. Colin turned and walked away but the music and the sound of Sylvia's laughter rang in his ears long after he could no longer hear them.

Helen Anthony stared disapprovingly at her daughter. 'Fanny, I *do* wish you'd do your homework somewhere else. You can't possibly concentrate properly sitting in front of the television with your books perched on your knee like that.'

'Look, it's bad enough having to do it at all without being banished to some dark cell,' retorted Fanny.

'Don't exaggerate.'

'Well, it *seems* like that. God, I've been doing school work

98

since nine o'clock this morning and it's half past nine at night now and I'm still not finished. If I didn't watch telly a bit I'd get completely cut off from real life. Ken says one must differentiate between education and mere training.'

'Oh, *Ken*!' Helen flapped a dismissive hand. 'That's all we ever hear from you these days, Fanny. Ken this, Ken that. Anyone would think he was the ultimate fount of truth and wisdom.'

'He's a damn sight truer and wiser than those silly women at school!' said Fanny hotly. 'They don't *want* to know what's true! They've got a fantasy world, all full of nice quiet brainy girls who don't think about sex. Here, what d'you think Mrs Newley said the other day? She came in to take the register looking all smug. "I have just seen a girl who shall be nameless", she said, "kissing a boy outside the launderette. Passionately. And I said to her, I said, a time and a place for everything, dear – don't you agree with me, girls?" Agree with her? She's got to be joking. We all knew who it was, anyway. It was Susan Weston. She and Mark have been around for ages. I mean, they're really *serious*.'

'I should think they must be,' said Stewart. 'Anyone who can be passionate outside a launderette at nine o'clock in the morning has my deepest admiration.'

'Quite,' said Fanny. 'But wasn't it *rude* of Mrs Newley! She wouldn't have spoken to a girl she didn't know. It was just because she's a teacher and she couldn't stop being a teacher outside school.'

'I'm inclined to agree,' said Stewart. 'I was thinking the other day how nice it would be if everyone could do something quite different for – say – six months every five years. Teachers should be pushed off to be plumbers' mates and doctors would go and work in factories. . . .'

'And who would do the teachers' jobs, then?' inquired Helen ironically. 'Truck drivers, I suppose? Or hairdressers?'

'Why not?' Stewart was unrepentant. 'Most educational. I'd love to put a great hairy truck driver in my consulting room and watch the results. He'd either say, " 'orspital for you, mate" or "stop in bed for a coupla days". Either way he wouldn't do much harm.'

'Honestly, Stewart, sometimes you're just plain silly,' said Helen.

Stewart gazed at her consideringly. 'I know what your three months should be,' he said. 'You can work on an assembly line, tying mauve ribbons round bottles of eau de cologne.'

'Oh, no – painting plaster ducks to put on the wall!' said Fanny. And Dominic joined in. 'Sticking the eyelashes on dollies!'

'Then you four,' said Helen icily, 'can be housewives. At three months each, that lets me out completely. *Good.*'

Stewart laughed. The game had gone far enough. 'How about a cup of coffee?' he said.

'Cocoa,' said Dominic.

'Me, too,' said Matthew.

Stewart got to his feet but Helen was already on her way to the door. 'No, no, Helen, I'll get it.'

Helen glared. 'I will *not* be made to feel guilty,' she said.

Fanny smiled to herself as she ruled a line under her completed homework. 'I'd like cocoa, too!' she called after her retreating mother and, when glared at, added, 'please, Helen!' Then she stuffed her books into the off-licence carrier bag which she intended to use as a satchel tomorrow and settled back in her chair. Now she could give her full attention to her favourite occupation – thinking about Ken.

Lee Haynes sat sprawled in Mary's rexine-covered armchair. He had been sitting in it for some time and he was now on his fourth cigarette. He shifted his position impatiently, swinging both legs up over the arm of the chair. In so doing, he knocked off the saucer which Mary had provided as an ashtray.

'Sorry,' he said, leaping up without reluctance to pick up butt-ends and scoop ineffectually at the insubstantial ash. 'Got a cloth?'

'Kleenex,' said Mary, unperturbed. 'On the dressing table.'

'Wish you'd hurry up with that blooming marking,' grumbled

Lee. 'I could take you out for a drink.'

'I don't want a drink,' said Mary primly, entering a B+ against Diane Purdie's name in her mark book.

Lee finished cleaning up the spilt ash, threw the used Kleenex in the waste-paper basket and sat down rather noisily at the table beside Mary.

'Got jam on it, these kids!' he said, riffling through the pile of exercise books. '*We* never had teachers like you. Not one decent pair of legs among the lot except the PE mistress – and she only taught the girls. Wasted, she was. Hey, that's funny!' He held up the exercise book he had arrived at. 'Fanny Anthony – d'you teach her?'

'Yes. Why?'

'Well, I know that kid!' After nearly an hour of bored silence the small coincidence excited Lee more than it warranted. 'She goes to the Theatre Centre. Great little actress, you know. You've seen her act, have you?'

'No, I haven't – well, I've only been in the school a few weeks. You never told me you were an actor, Lee!'

'Me?' Lee laughed. 'Gerraway! No, I don't tread the old boards. I do the electrics. Wire 'em up for effects and all that. Thunderstorms, volcanoes – you name it, I'll do it. Always fancied stage electrics as a full-time job, but you have to be lucky, don't you?'

For the first time that evening, Mary gave Lee her full attention. 'Now, isn't that interesting,' she said. 'I had no idea there was a Theatre Centre in this town – I mean, it's such a stuffy place, isn't it?'

'You can say that again,' agreed Lee. 'Look – tell you what, you finish your marking and I'll take you down to the Centre. You can meet a few people, see what goes on – and we'll nip in for a quickie at the Five Bells on the way home. How's that?'

'That sounds lovely,' said Mary, warmed by Lee's unexpected interests. 'Two more books to do and I'll be with you.'

'Great!' said Lee. The evening had been a dead loss so far – he had wired up two plugs and spent an hour in that bloody armchair – but it looked as if it might pay off, after all.

Mary found everything at the Theatre Centre wholly delightful. She was not in the least bit put off by loose floorboards in two of the dressing rooms or the large damp patch on the ceiling of the green room kitchen. 'It's got such a marvellous *feel*,' she said. 'I mean, you could do anything here, couldn't you? It's a proper working place.'

Lee conducted her round with off-hand pride, opening doors and indicating the contents of the room with disparaging familiarity. 'And this horrible little cupboard,' he would say, 'is what we laughingly call the Wardrobe. Oh, sorry, Mrs Lovegrove. Thought you was a moth.'

Coming down the steep, lino-clad stairs they encountered the Senior Section chattering and gesticulating their way out of the auditorium.

'Actors,' said Lee with contempt. 'Raving nutters, most of them. Good thing that lot have gone – now you can see the stage before the pubs close.'

As he pushed open the black baize-covered door, the sound of a piano met them. Slightly out of tune, the lazy, rhythmic, tinkling notes held for Mary all the timeless magic of the theatre. The tune was as tired and as sweet as faded violets; it was disillusioned and self-mocking and yet it conjured up an indestructible gaiety. 'We said – we'd never look back,' sang the pianist in a husky, rather tuneless tenor. With a couple of chirpy chords he finished the number, stood up and looked across the top of the piano.

'ʹEvening, Lee,' he said. 'And who is this lovely mad girl? For mad she must be, to come here with you.'

'Give over,' said Lee. 'This is Mary Ross. Mary, this horrible man is Ken Olliphant and he's OK as long as you keep him at arm's length and don't believe a word he says.'

Ken gazed at Lee reproachfully. 'And what, little Sparky, have I ever done to you?' he inquired. Not waiting for an answer, he turned to Mary. 'One has to associate with such *funny* people,' he confided.

'Oh, one does,' agreed Mary with a glance at Lee, who did not smile. 'You should see some of the people I work with!'

she added hastily. 'We've got one who fusses about what colour rubber bands the girls wear to tie their hair back.'

'Ah! Rubber band fetishism!' said Ken. 'Filth strikes again. So you are in the teaching trade, my dear?'

Mary nodded. 'I teach English at Critchlowe's.'

Ken stared at her gravely. 'Forgive me if I am impertinent, but why did you go and teach there?'

Mary found herself blushing. 'Well, why not? I just applied for a post advertised in the *Times Ed. Supp.* – I mean, it sounded quite a nice school.'

'Oh, it is, it is. That's just the point. Schools like that are too nice to breathe. But is it *good*? Do the kids think or do they just concentrate on being nice?'

'The girls *I* teach think,' said Mary hotly, 'or I'll want to know the reason why.'

'Brave words,' said Ken. 'How long have you been teaching?'

'About three weeks,' admitted Mary, and laughed.

Lee, who had listened to this conversation with increasing impatience, put his fingers in his mouth and blew an ear-splitting whistle. 'School's over! Play-time!' He glared at Ken with mock fury. 'Bloody menace you are, Olliphant. I brought this girl out for a drink, not for an educational conference.' He took Mary by the arm. 'Come on, love, or they'll close.'

'What about Ken?' said Mary. 'Can't you join us, Ken? I'm sure Lee won't mind.'

'I'm sure Lee will,' said Ken with a grin. 'But I'm coming all the same.' He held the door open for her and she smiled up at him as she went through.

Lee followed them gloomily. This was going to cost him a pint of Guinness for bloody Ken and the girl would no doubt want some fancy thing like a Campari soda and what did yours truly get out of it? Sweet Fanny Adams.

3 Wednesday

'You shouldn't have got up, Mum,' said Marjorie. 'There was no need. I could have seen Bobbie off to school.'

Bobbie smiled but said nothing. Today made two mornings running for her mother. Quite a record.

Sylvia, huddled in her dressing gown, made a deprecatory gesture with her cigarette and took another sip of tea. Her face was the colour of uncooked pastry.

Gordon came in from putting the cot on to the car's roof rack. 'Better get going if you've got to work this morning,' he said.

Marjorie made a face. 'Unfortunately, yes,' she said. 'I rang Mr Carter to see if he could do without me but Linda's still off with a sore throat that only leaves Mrs Amery to do the two surgeries *and* reception.'

Sylvia closed her eyes. 'If you have to go,' she said, 'you have to go. Spare me the excuses.'

Keron, perched on two cushions at the breakfast table, began to bang his cereal bowl rhythmically with his spoon. Sylvia leaned across the table and snatched the spoon out of his hand.

'Want spoon!' shouted Keron. 'Want spoon, want spoon!'

Sylvia put her hand to her head and said, 'For Christ's sake shut him up.'

Marjorie picked the little boy up and took him across to the sink where she wiped his hands and face. 'We're going in the car,' she said. 'Going to nursery. You like nursery, don't you?'

Keron gave a high-pitched squeal of delight. Sylvia flinched.

'Oh, come on,' said Gordon. 'Kids and hangovers don't mix.

Let's get off. Can we drop you at school, Bob?' He paused. 'Bobbie?'

'What?' Bobbie came to with a start.

'Lift,' snapped Sylvia. 'Wake *up*, girl!'

'Oh. Yes, thank you very much.'

'What about the washing up, Mum?' asked Marjorie. 'Shall I put it in the machine for you?'

'No, thank you,' said Sylvia heavily.

'Oh. Well, if you're sure. Coat on, then, Keron.'

'I'm going back to bed,' said Sylvia.

'That's a good idea, Mum,' said Marjorie. 'I'll ring you this evening to see how Dad is. You're not going to the hospital today, are you?'

'They didn't seem to want me,' said Sylvia.

'Never mind – just you relax.'

'Try two Alka Seltzers and a can of orange juice,' advised Gordon. 'Now, come on, you lot. It's nearly quarter past eight and I won't be at work until ten as it is.'

Sylvia turned at the door. 'I am sorry,' she said, 'to be such a nuisance.' And she went out.

'Always got a good exit line, old Sylvia,' said Gordon, with a grin.

'Why don't you put the bags in the car,' said Marjorie coldly, 'if you're in such a hurry.'

Bobbie slid everything out of focus. Cold air blew in through the front door as she stood beside her basket of books and stared at the wallpaper opposite. It was a pattern of interlocking squares which made her mind feel like a mouse in a maze. You could run along the mud-brown right-angled roads for a limited time and then you either came back to the place where you had started or else you had to cross a black line to start on the silver-grey roads system. Either way it was frustrating.

'Come on, Dolly Daydream,' said Marjorie's voice in her ear, 'we're all waiting for you.'

Bobbie was the last one out of the house. Before she shut the door, she called up the stairs, 'Bye, Mum!' She listened – but there was no answer.

Bobbie enjoyed being in the car. Gordon had been revving it up for so long that the heater was already blowing warm air, and the radio was playing pop music.

'Do we *have* to have Radio One?' asked Marjorie from the back seat as they started off. 'It's just *noise*.'

Gordon prodded the tuning button and the music changed to a Viennese waltz. 'Oh, *The Merry Widow*!' said Marjorie. 'That's better!'

Irresistibly, Bobbie visualised a neat, jet-black figure, dancing until dawn crept through the long windows of the ballroom. Black eyes glancing from behind a fan and a dead husband in the earth. Oh, no. Why this stupid obsession with death and awfulness? Dad would be all right. Sister Davis said so.

'Where's this school of yours, Bobbie?' asked Gordon. 'Not down one of those unmade roads, is it?'

'I'm afraid so,' said Bobbie. 'Next on the left. But just drop me on the corner and I'll walk down. I always do, from the bus stop.'

'Don't be soft. This one, is it?'

'Yes.' The radio was playing *Country Gardens*.

Gordon slowed for the corner and the car's automatic gearbox changed ratios once and then twice, then, as he started along the gravelled road at a slower pace, back again once.

'Dad says he doesn't like automatic cars,' said Bobbie. 'I don't know why. I think they're terribly clever.'

'Ah, well, he's a sporty driver, isn't he?' said Gordon ironically. ' 'Course, he may not be so sporty after this little lot. Good thing too. He drives like a bloody maniac. God, these roads are terrible. Why doesn't the Council make them up?'

'Something to do with Critchlowe's Fields Estate,' said Bobbie. 'It's still private land or something.'

' "Fields" is the word! You need a tractor along here, not a car. Christ, is that it?'

'Yes.'

Gordon brought the car to a halt and gazed at the school with astonished amusement. 'It's a cross between Buck House and Wormwood Scrubs, isn't it!' he said. 'Abandon hope all ye who enter here!'

'That's what Fanny says,' said Bobbie. 'How does this seat belt go? I don't quite. . . .'

Gordon released her and opened the door. 'What about going home?' he asked. 'Will Sylvia want you back early, do you think? I *might* be able to get off work and give you a lift. . . .'

'You can't really promise, though, Gordon,' said Marjorie from the back seat.

'It's all right,' said Bobbie, getting out, 'I usually walk home with Fanny, anyway.'

'Don't forget your basket,' said Gordon.

'Oh, thank you. I almost did. Bye-bye, Keron!' She waved, and the little boy waved back with both hands. Bobbie shut the car door ineffectually on the first click and Gordon shut it again.

'Hang on,' said Marjorie. 'I'm coming in the front.'

As his wife transferred herself, Gordon watched Bobbie go in through the iron gate. She looked smaller, somehow, and with that white face – Gordon felt a pang of conscience about not picking her up later on. It was easy enough to leave early – old Cummings didn't mind.

'Right,' said Marjorie. 'Off we go.'

And Gordon duly went.

Mary Ross arrived at school early and went into the staff room feeling unusually cheerful. The room was empty except for Iris Newley, who stood warming her outspread hands over the electric kettle.

'Good morning!' said Mary gaily, 'isn't it a gorgeous day!'

Iris did not answer and Mary, glancing at her in some surprise, perceived a slight, convulsive aversion of the older woman's head and knew that Iris Newley was crying.

'What's the matter?' she asked gently. 'Can I help?'

Iris struggled to retain control. 'My dog,' she said tightly. 'Found him dead this morning.' She gave a loud, hiccuping sob and shook her head, angry with her weakness.

Mary felt helpless. In a few minutes, however, Mrs Newley blew her nose loudly and said, 'Sorry to be such a fool. Shouldn't get so fond of an animal but he was all I'd got, you see.' Her face quivered but she busied herself pouring the boiling water from the kettle into the big teapot and when she spoke again she sounded her usual tough self. 'Be a dear and pour out the tea when the others arrive, will you?'

'Yes, of course,' said Mary.

Mrs Newley, red-eyed, turned at the door of the staff cloakroom and added, 'Perhaps Miss Perkins would take my register for me. A face like this and a class like 4N simply don't mix.'

Half in pity and half in admiration, Mary smiled. 'I'll ask her,' she said.

Bobbie pushed her way into the crowded cloakroom, took off her blazer and hung it on her peg. Cloakrooms, she thought, were one of the nastiest things about school. There was something so awful about the apportioned peg, wire basket and bench space – like a battery hen house. Or Buchenwald. The documentary film she had seen years ago yawned horribly into Bobbie's mind; the barbed wire arching over on goose-necked supports; the dreadful doors that swung open along the length of a blackened brick building, each one supporting an obscene cradle, each one closing into a furnace. Oh, the deliberate, efficient mechanisms of death and disposal, all neat and clanking and horrible!

Bobbie sat down on the wooden bench, overwhelmed by mental nausea. The smell of plimsolls and sweat and wet concrete poured in through her mouth and nose and seeped through her brain.

The wire mesh, hung with blazers like a game-keeper's gibbet, hurt her eyes. Everything, everything was hard and cold and unkind.

Suddenly Bobbie remembered the dead blue tit she had found when she was very small. It was not long dead, for it was soft and not at all bedraggled. Its eyes were peacefully closed and its matchstick-thin legs ended in loosely curled claws. Its plumage, lemon yellow, forget-me-not and indigo, was unruffled and brilliant. Bobbie had picked it up, cradling it carefully in her hands, and taken it into the house. Sylvia had uttered a scream and turned her face away and Bobbie's father, giving no indication of his intentions, had picked the bird out of her hands by one leg and dropped it into the kitchen boiler.

Remembering how she had attacked her father, hitting at him and screaming at his destruction of her pretty bird, Bobbie's pulse beat faster. The flush of blood to her face made her aware again of Cloakroom D and of the bustle around her, which was abating a little as most people had already gone to their classrooms.

'Bobbie! Hello – you all right?' Fanny plumped herself down beside her friend. Instead of her cardboard box, Bobbie noticed, she had a plastic carrier from Wineways. She smiled. 'Is that your new briefcase?'

'That's right,' said Fanny. 'Neat and practical. Respectability, you see – gets us all in the end. How's your dad?'

'I don't know, really,' said Bobbie. 'The hospital didn't ring or anything. They said don't keep coming to see him while he's still unconscious. Oh, Fanny, he does look ghastly, I can't tell you. Sorry I was so sort of un-talking last night. I just wasn't with it.'

' 'Course you weren't,' said Fanny. 'What about your mum – is she very upset?'

Bobbie did not want to think about Sylvia. 'She's gone back to bed,' she said.

Fanny sniffed. Then she said, 'Did Colin come round last night? Sandie – er – happened to mention he went out and I just thought....'

'No,' said Bobbie, turning pink. 'I mean, yes, he did come but I'd gone to sleep. Marjorie told me this morning.'

'He's nice, isn't he?'

'Yes, he's very nice.' Bobbie had carefully not thought about Colin yet this morning. With Gordon and Marjorie bustling about and Sylvia glowering, there was no privacy to think about anything as exciting and frightening as Colin.

'Do you like him, Bob?' pursued Fanny inquisitively.

'Yes. I told you, he's very nice.' Bobbie's small face was closed and guarded. Fanny laughed. 'Oh, all right. No need to go all uptight, I can see you're bats about him. Hey, I like that jumper you're wearing. Is that the one I got out of the shoe bag yesterday?'

'Yes. I couldn't find my cardigan this morning so I just put it on. I must give it back, though. Do you know which bag it came from?'

'No idea. It'll be marked, though. We can find out easily enough. You'll have to wear it for today, until you find your cardigan.'

'I expect Mrs Webb will find it. She comes today.'

'Good. Here, we'd better go. Bell went ages ago.'

'Did it?' Bobbie scrambled to her feet. 'Oh, Fanny, every-one's gone, look. I am an idiot – fancy just sitting here all that time. I was so early too, because Gordon gave me a lift.'

'Not to panic. Ma Newley knows all about you going home, so she won't be too tough. Gosh, I didn't tell you about the row yesterday, did I? You know how it's always bloody this and damn that with the Newley bird – I mean, *everybody* does it, but with her it's somehow deliberate – well, we really had a go about it. . . .'

Bobbie could not get Fanny to hurry. The prospect of trouble in store, she reflected, always brought out the worst in Fanny. Instead of trying to minimise it, she always went straight at it head first.

'Do come on, Fanny,' she said. 'We really are awfully late.'

Fanny, interrupted in her monologue, looked pained. She adopted a wooden-legged limp and groaned, 'It's me books. It's this terrible 'eavy weight of learning what's weighing me down. You run along, my dear.' Her voice became increasingly peevish and toothless as the part grew on her. 'Don't you waste your time waiting for us old 'uns. Now I've got me leg-irons I can 'obble along a treat in me own sweet time. No, don't you wait, dear. You run along a'ead.'

But Bobbie, convulsed with giggles, did wait, and knew that she always would.

Sylvia Rippon, for the second time that morning, got reluctantly out of bed. Since her family's departure, sleep had obstinately eluded her and Gordon's light-hearted advice about orange juice and Alka Seltzer had prodded insistently at her buzzing head and parched throat. She put on her dressing gown and made her way carefully down to the kitchen.

Ignoring the milk bottles and coffee cups and Keron's half-eaten cornflakes, Sylvia raised the lid of the deep freeze, hoping to find a can of concentrated orange juice. She was confronted by three gallon-sized tins of ice-cream (chocolate, vanilla and strawberry) and a large cardboard box which contained nine kilos of frozen peas. But there was no orange juice.

Sylvia slammed the freezer lid shut. Her thirst was becoming serious, a gritty dehydration which made her feel shrunken inside. She drank a little water from the tap but its flat taste was repulsive, like the smell of an old face flannel. She needed something sharp and refreshing. She went into the sitting room where the curtains were still drawn and, in the sour, ashy-smelling half-darkness, went across to the cocktail cabinet. She took out two bottles of tonic water and a clean glass then, after a second's hesitation, a bottle of vodka. She closed the cabinet and groped her way back across the dark room, accidentally kicking over a half-full glass of Martini which someone had left on the floor. The thought of mopping up the spilt drink from the carpet made her head throb – and anyway, Mrs Webb would be here soon.

Holding her bottles and glass very carefully, Sylvia climbed up the stairs and, once again, went back to bed.

Bobbie peered through the slit of glass which was all that was not obscured by a wallchart pinned on the inside of the door, then turned to Fanny, her face aghast.

'It's Miss *Perkins*!'

'Oh, Lord. Now we're for it.'

'Fanny, I can't. She's so awful and she goes on and on at you, I *can't* go in there, honestly I can't!'

'Ssh! Don't let her hear you. Look, she won't eat you. Come on. I'll make some excuse.'

But Bobbie was in a complete panic. 'I'm not going in, Fanny, I'm not. I'll be sick.'

Fanny thought quickly. 'Go back to the cloakroom, then. I'll tell her you've been sick in the loo and you'll be in for first lesson – OK? I'll bring your books.'

Bobbie nodded, white faced. Then she turned and half-walked, half-ran back along the empty corridor to the stairs. Fanny watched her until she turned the corner then, without bothering to prepare any mental defences, opened the classroom door and walked in.

'Ah!' Miss Perkins swivelled round in her chair in order to direct the full blast of her attention upon Fanny. 'Miss Anthony.' She looked Fanny up and down very slowly while the class tittered disloyally.

'I'm sorry I'm late,' began Fanny, 'but....'

Miss Perkins held up her hand. 'I am not ready for your string of feeble excuses yet.' Her voice measured out its sarcasms. 'Stand still and let us all see this Fanny Anthony who is so superior that she is above the rules which govern the rest of us. M'm. I should have thought that someone who fancies herself as an actress would take a little more interest in her appearance. You would look pleasanter with your hair tied back as the school regulations require. And black tights with a ladder in them look utterly squalid. Your blouse is not clean and your skirt is quite disgusting.'

'It got splashed when I was washing up. I....'

'How dare you interrupt me! I have spoken to you before about finding a proper satchel or briefcase for your books. That bag is a deliberate, calculated insult, as is your whole appearance and manner. Where is your tie?'

'At home.'

'At home,' repeated Miss Perkins with contemptuous gaze. 'At home. Do you mean to imply that your mother condones your deliberate flouting of the school rules? Did she *see* you go out this morning?'

'I don't know.'

'What do you mean, you don't know?'

'Well, my father had to go out to an emergency – someone with a coronary, he thought – and there were a lot of phone calls. Helen takes them until the receptionist comes in at eight-thirty. So she was sort of in and out.'

'And who, may I ask, is Helen?'

'My mother.'

'I see.' Miss Perkins' lip curled. 'One of these modern families. So nobody cares whether you go to school or not, is that it?'

'No, that is *not* it!' shouted Fanny, her temper flaring uncontrollably at this injustice. 'You can just stop talking about my family because it's *me* that's here, not them, and it's *me* that's responsible.'

Miss Perkins unexpectedly smiled, thus effectively taking the wind out of Fanny's sails. 'Dear, dear,' she remarked mildly, 'we *are* in an emotional state this morning, aren't we? And where is your little friend?'

Fanny felt like a bull that has just charged past the matador without managing to touch him.

'She's been sick,' she said sulkily.

'Sick where? At home? At school?'

'At school.'

'Then where is she now? Don't sulk, Fanny. You are continually either showing off or sulking. Is Roberta present or not?'

'Yes, she is. I said I'd get her books for her and she'll be here for first lesson.'

'I see.' Miss Perkins marked both girls present but late and totalled the register. Then she sat back. 'You, Fanny, will come to detention tomorrow after school in the small hall. You will also report to me in my room at ten to nine tomorrow morning wearing brown tights and a clean school uniform, including your tie. And your hair will be tied *back*, do you understand?'

'Yes, Miss Perkins,' said Fanny promptly, with just a shade

too much parade-ground efficiency in her voice. This was not lost on Miss Perkins, who turned on her with a flash of real anger.

'What you *are*, Fanny,' she said, tight-lipped, 'is outside my control, thank goodness. What you *do*, however, affects in some small way every single person in this school. It is people like you, disruptive, cynical people, who cause all the trouble in the world. Society must be protected from those that threaten it and while I am a member of this staff, Fanny Anthony, I shall see that this school is protected from you. Go and sit down.'

I'm *not* an enemy of society, I'm *not*, cried Fanny to herself, badly shaken by Miss Perkins' attack. Behind the shelter of desk lids she packed books for the morning's lessons for herself and Bobbie, hoping that she looked as unconcerned as she would like to appear. Thank goodness Bobbie had fled to the cloakroom! If she, Fanny, felt so upset, whatever would the effect have been on Bobbie? The other girls, murmuring to each other in low voices, eyed Fanny covertly. Some, like Sandie McIver, sent nods of sympathy but the others watched her with smug curiosity. They were, Fanny thought, like the people who gawp at an accident, morbidly fascinated by the injury and pain which is not theirs. At least, not this time.

Downstairs in the cloakroom, Bobbie sat huddled on a bench, her arms clutched round her knees. The sense of desolation which overwhelmed her was frightening. She sat sideways to the wall pressed against the cold, cream-painted brickwork in the scanty shelter of two gabardine raincoats. She felt a desperate need for refuge.

I hate it, said Bobbie silently. I hate this place. All of it.

The admission was unexpectedly sad. The routine of school life gave a certain pattern to each day and it was possible sometimes to feel a sense of belonging to a group – but only at a price. The group liked people who fitted in neatly. In order to belong, each individual had to sense what the group expected and then try to perform accordingly. Some were lucky and seemed to fit naturally; others, like Fanny, were strong enough to accept its benefits and ignore its pressures. But many had to strike a bargain, assuming a pretended personality for the security of 'belonging'. Bobbie, huddled on her bench, was too tired to make any such effort. The 4N group was essentially energetic, aggressive and flippant in style. Bitchiness was admired whereas sincerity was regarded as an embarrassment. Wit was appreciated but criticism was a bore; humour was acceptable only if it was based on a universally understood code, and originality, like garlic, was only tolerable in minute quantities.

No, the 4N group was not for the weary or the faint at heart. And the other group, the godlike Staff, were equally demanding. They had to be propitiated with good behaviour and high standards.

Bobbie put her head on her knees and closed her eyes. Unexpectedly, she found that she was longing to see Colin. Her memory of him, slight though it was, was illuminated by a warm sense of trust. She thought of his hands gripping her arms as she had collided with him on the footbridge, and of his grave courtesy when he had returned the basket of books to her. His eyes were a clear grey, with dark lashes, and his hair was very beautiful, a deep, browny-red colour, and wavy. And he had come to see her last night. Now *nice* of him.

Bobbie felt a sudden access of determination. She uncurled her legs and got off the bench to go up and join her class in the biology lab for the first lesson.

In the door of the cloakroom she came face to face with Mrs Cox, who taught PE. Mrs Cox was a small woman, hardly taller than Bobbie herself, but built with rubbery solidity. She was wearing a maroon-coloured track suit and had a whistle on a length of red braid round her neck. Under one arm she carried a netball.

'What are you doing in here?' she said sharply.

'I – I wasn't feeling well.' Bobbie tried to edge past but the PE mistress put her hand across the doorway, barring her exit.

'Just you wait a minute,' she said, narrowing her blue eyes suspiciously. 'What's your name?'

'Roberta Rippon.'

'Form?'

'4N.'

'Why are you wearing that sweater?'

Bobbie blushed guiltily, not realising the comparatively innocent cause of the question.

'Sweaters are supposed to be V-necked,' went on Mrs Cox,
'*not* round-necked. You're the second girl I've had to – oho!' A
new thought had struck her. 'I suppose that is *your* sweater, is
it?'

'Well – not exactly, but I—'

'You pinched it from a shoe bag in the gym cloakroom
yesterday, didn't you!' said Mrs Cox triumphantly. 'Take it
off.'

'But—'

'Take it *off*!'

Sick with apprehension, Bobbie peeled the sweater over
her head. Mrs Cox snatched it and inspected the name tape
sewn into the neck, then pushed it at Bobbie, indicating the
tape with a weather-reddened finger.

'Veronica Downes. So, you nasty little thief, I suppose you've
been sneaking round this cloakroom too, have you, looking for
something else that takes your fancy!'

'I haven't, I haven't!' Bobbie burst into tears. 'I *didn't* take
it!'

'Who did, then?'

Bobbie shook her head blindly. She could not say that Fanny
had taken it, because that was not true either – not in the way
that Mrs Cox meant. And Fanny would be in enough trouble
already, being late for registration when Miss Perkins was
there.

'You seem to be a liar as well as a thief,' said Mrs Cox.
'You're coming straight up to see Miss Perkins.'

'No!' screamed Bobbie. 'No, I won't!' She twisted her arm
away from Mrs Cox's restraining grasp and fled through the
cloakroom to the door which led out to the yard. Mrs Cox, still
holding the round-necked sweater, started after Bobbie in pur-

suit but caught her foot on the basket of books which Bobbie had abandoned on the floor. By the time she had recovered her balance Bobbie was out of the door, which she pulled shut behind her with such panic-stricken violence that one of its windows was shattered by the impact. The crash and tinkle of broken glass added the last impetus of terror to Bobbie's flight. She tore headlong round the side of the building and down the path, out of the gate and away along the gravelled road. Mrs Cox lost sight of Bobbie. By the time she had circum-navigated the broken glass and run round to the path, there was no girl to be seen. The PE mistress stared up and down the road, her pink face puckered with worry. There was no way of telling which direction Bobbie had taken.

What was she to do now? If the girl had really run away from school then she would have to report it. The pupils were the school's responsibility during school hours. On the other hand, if Roberta came sneaking back – which she very probably would – then Mrs Cox was going to look very silly for having raised an unnecessary alarm. After all, there was no reason why anyone should know about the incident. Mrs Cox wondered uneasily whether her attempt to detain the girl had left the weals of fingernails on her arm, but consoled herself with the thought that Roberta was at least an undoubted thief. The round-necked sweater marked with another girl's name remained to prove it.

Meanwhile, there was a class waiting on the netball court. Roberta Rippon, Mrs Cox decided, could wait until lunch time. Wherever she was.

Fanny, keeping an anxious eye on the door for Bobbie's reappearance, cursed the fact that biology was a double period lesson. There would be no break at five to ten for lesson change, during which she could have nipped down to the cloakroom.

Finally, she put up her hand.

'Yes, what *is* it, Fanny?' Miss Armstrong hated interruptions.

'Could I go and see what's happened to Bobbie, please? She said she wasn't feeling well and. . . .'

117

'No, certainly not. If she isn't well then she'll be in the medical room or she may have been sent home. In either case, it's nothing to do with you.'

Fanny glowered. She should have simply asked to be excused. There would have been an embarrassing fuss about 'seeing to that kind of thing before you arrive' and everyone would have giggled, but she would have got out.

Where *was* Bobbie?

Bobbie ran until she was too out of breath to run any further. She jogged to a walk and then sat down on a low concrete pillar at the entrance to one of the sports grounds. She had run in the direction least known to her, away from the town across the Critchlowe's Fields estate and was now near the railway station.

As her pounding heart gradually slackened its pace, Bobbie became aware that there was quite a brisk wind blowing. Deprived by Mrs Cox of the round-necked sweater and without her blazer, Bobbie began to feel cold. She stood up and started to walk again, with a sour, burning taste in her throat from having run so far.

She went through the subway which led underneath the railway line and came out in Denmark Street, which led eventually to the far end of Wilmot Road. She paused, undecided what to do. She could not go back to school and face their anger. The broken window, the stolen sweater, being late for registration, getting Fanny to lie for her – and now, on top of it all, playing truant. She would be expelled. There was no doubt about it. Whatever would her mother say?

'To do this to me *now*, Bobbie, when I am so alone, a poor widow struggling to make ends meet. . . .'

Bobbie gave a sudden gasp of horror, superstitiously aware of her fatal assumption. Widow. Merry Widow. She had let the idea creep into her head that her father had died, and she had made no defences against it, raised no protecting reality, crossed no fingers. Did she *want* her father to die? No, no, of course not, it wasn't true, it was a threat which could still be warded off, still be thought away out of existence. Her father was going to be perfectly all right, Sister Davis had said so.

A passing woman stared at Bobbie and she realised that she must present an odd appearance, standing irresolute and coatless in a busy shopping parade, hugging herself to keep warm in her white blouse and navy skirt. What an obvious fugitive! The school would ring up the police. At any moment a squad car might pull up beside her. 'Get in' they would say grimly, and all the shopping women would stare as she was bundled into the car and driven away, back to school – oh, no. Not back to school. If only she had something to put on over her uniform, or a different coloured skirt.... 'Get yourself a new skirt'.

Of course! Only yesterday morning her mother had given Bobbie a five pound note – or had she dreamed it? Bobbie felt in the small pocket in the waistband of her skirt. Three dinner tickets and – yes – a tightly folded note. It really was there. Wonderful.

With a new sense of purpose, Bobbie walked along the parade, glancing into the windows in search of the shop she wanted. 'Maureen, Ladies' Fashions' – no. That was no good. The dummies in the window were all of the silver-haired, smiling sort, wearing dresses and two-piece suits, all in shades of autumn brown. Bobbie walked on, and came at last to a large, neon-lit shop with Dayglo pink, yellow and green price cards in its windows, which were crammed with jeans, underwear and piles of knitting wool. Inside the open doors stood wire baskets full of basketball boots and interlock vests, slight seconds. It seemed the ideal place. Bobbie went in.

Her attention was at once caught by some fluffy short-sleeved jumpers in electric colours but she dismissed them sternly from consideration. She needed something inconspicuous and practical; something which would cover up as much as possible of her school uniform while keeping out the cold wind. And, if possible, it would leave her some change from the five pounds. Bobbie decided on a long zip-fronted cardigan with a belt, knitted in a thick cable stitch and coloured olive green, labelled, 'Manufacturer's Second, £3.75.' It was a shame, she thought, to spend so much money on such a dull garment, but this was an emergency. She paid for the cardigan and went out of the shop with it in a large paper bag. She shivered a little in her cotton blouse and wished she had had the courage to put the cardigan on in the shop. But a girl in school uniform buying a garment which she immediately put on might well be remembered by even the dimmest of shop assistants. 'Oh, yes, constable, that's the girl all right, I'd know her anywhere....' But how was she to get the cardigan out of the bag without attracting attention?

The problem solved itself easily. Bobbie came to a park and turned in through the tall gates to walk between the rhododendron bushes bordering the tarmac path until she came to a sign which said 'Ladies'. Of course!

In the blissfully private cubicle, Bobbie put on the cardigan and stuffed the tightly crumpled paper bag into the plastic bin which stood in the corner. Then she took off her tell-tale school tie and wound it into a tight roll. Where could she hide it? In the bin? Some cleaner might notice it. With some distaste, Bobbie retrieved the paper bag which had contained her cardigan, pushed the tie into it and threw it back into the bin. Feeling horribly guilty, she washed her hands quickly and fled.

The warmth of the olive green cardigan was consoling and Bobbie walked through the park with growing calmness, comforted by her anonymity. She looked at her watch. Five past eleven. It would be morning break time at school. Fanny, at least, would know that she had run away. What would she think? That Bobbie had gone home? Yes, of course. Miss Beacon would think so, too, when she found out, as she inevitably would. Five past eleven. That left five hours and twenty minutes before school ended. It was a long time to fill. Perhaps she could go home as they all expected. Mrs Webb would be there, beady-eyed and unsmiling. 'Sent you home, have they? Been taken ill?' She was difficult to lie to, shrewd and hard-boiled. And Sylvia. What could she say to Sylvia?

Bobbie sighed. No, she would not go home. At four o'clock or thereabouts, when her presence would attract no suspicion, she would go to Fanny's house. Fanny, at least, deserved an explanation. Until then – what? But then, what did other people do all day who did not work? What of the retired people who lived in little boarding houses? What of the ladies of leisure who filled their time with embroidery and gossip? For today, Bobbie was a lady of leisure. She giggled at the idea, walking along the demure paths with their neatly patterned iron hoops fencing off the flower beds.

The park was changing in character from a faintly *Midsummer Night's Dream* setting with bosky bushes and discreet benches to a more formal area where litter bins sprouted at regular intervals along the neat verges. Bobbie came to an immense Boy Scout's badge made of close-packed tiny plants and gazed at it in fascination. It was fiercely clipped and presented a surface as uniform as a cut moquette sofa. It was edged by a minuscule version of privet, yellow-leafed and horribly tiny. A cigarette packet lay near Bobbie's feet and, in a sudden gesture of defiance, she picked it up and lobbed it on to the absurd badge. It landed at the left-hand point of the fleur de lis. Dissatisfied, Bobbie found a lolly stick and threw that as well. If Fanny had been there, she thought, she'd have been digging in the litter bin by now, in full cry for more ammunition. It was a very Fannyish thing to do. The lolly stick had landed across the middle of the motto, 'Be Prepared' spelled out in blodgy tufts of thyme. It looked disgusting. With one of her abrupt changes of mood, Bobbie felt guilty. What a grubby little act of vandalism. She stepped over the iron hoops on to the narrow strip of grass and reached out as far as she could to try and retrieve her bits of rubbish. The lolly stick was easy enough but the cigarette packet was further away. The close-packed, tufty plants looked dense and tough enough to take just a little weight, though. Bobbie extended a hand and tested the surface. It felt strong and springy. She leaned on it a little, then a little more. She could almost reach the cigarette packet. . . .

With a crunch of rending twigs and a sudden, outraged smell of thyme, the Boy Scout badge collapsed under Bobbie's weight and she pitched face downwards into the prickly embrace of the fleur de lis.

''Ere!' bellowed a distant but rapidly approaching voice. 'Watcher think yer doin'?' Bobbie threshed about, trying to regain her feet in the tangle of stalks and leaves and then, shedding sprigs of small plants as she went, leaped out of the awful badge and, for the second time that morning, took to her heels.

'You come back 'ere!' The voice, Bobbie perceived, sounded cracked and breathless but she did not stop running until she had put the rose gardens, the bowling green and the Scented Garden for the Blind between herself and the pursuer. Then she slowed down and glanced round nervously. There was nobody in sight. Running away was a wonderfully simple solution to one's problems, she thought. She walked on past the beds of dahlias and down the sloping grass which led to the boating pool, and came to the children's playground. The little roundabouts stood motionless and the seesaws cocked one or other of their ends at the sky and the swings hung silently on their long chains, waiting to be set into motion. Bobbie, responding to an old-established passion, went over to the nearest swing. Designed for small children, it had a box arrangement instead of a seat; but its chains were beautifully long. Ideal for standing-up swinging. Bobbie stepped carefully into the little high-chair-like seat and, bending her knees, began to drive the swing into its first forward arc. When it was going high enough, she leaned back on fully-extended arms, her body as straight as a pendulum, and stared up into the grey, windy, rocking sky, raked across and back again by the swing's horizontal bar, until her ears hummed with the dizzying rhythm of her to-ing and fro-ing.

'I fully understand how you felt, Mrs Cox,' said Miss Beacon, 'and the business of the jersey needs to be looked into, of course – although we must not assume that she stole it without hearing her side of the story. I must remind you, though, that a memorandum about Roberta's father was pinned on the staff notice board yesterday afternoon. Did you not read it?'

'I'm afraid I didn't,' confessed Mrs Cox. 'There was a hockey match after school and I didn't come up to the staff room and this morning I went straight into the gym. And I was on yard duty at break. What did it say?'

'Mr Rippon was seriously injured in a car accident yesterday.'

'Oh, dear.'

'Oh dear, indeed. And you have allowed more than two hours to elapse before reporting the girl's absence.'

'I thought she'd come back.'

'A rash assumption. But we learn from experience, don't we?' Miss Beacon smiled kindly. Hating her, Mrs Cox smiled back. Miss Beacon continued to regard the PE mistress for a few minutes more. Then, remorselessly, she added, 'A teacher's mistakes, you see, are apt to be particularly damaging ones. You cannot discard your failures and start again. If we flatter ourselves that we have some effect, then we must be prepared to live with that effect.' She sat back. 'Now, I won't keep you any longer, Mrs Cox. I know you practical people have a lot of preparation to do.'

Dismissed, Mrs Cox said wretchedly, 'I really am awfully sorry about it, Miss Beacon.'

This time, Miss Beacon did not smile. 'I'm sure you are,' she said. And this time, Mrs Cox left the room.

As the door clicked shut, Miss Beacon mentally cursed the woman for her ineptitude. This was the kind of situation which was apt to give the school a bad name. And, of course, there was the question of the girl herself. Roberta was bound to be under some strain at present and her school career had in any case been punctuated by lapses into irrational behaviour. She had a tendency towards 'mental truancy' which several of the staff had noticed, but this generally resulted in mere dreaminess. Today's running away episode did not seem characteristic of the girl at all. Very probably she was simply worried about her father. After the upset with Mrs Cox she would have gone straight home to see if there was any news about him.

Miss Beacon buzzed her secretary and asked her to get Roberta Rippon's mother on the telephone.

Mrs Webb heard the telephone ringing and switched off the vacuum cleaner.

'Hello?'

'Hold the line, please – I have a call for you.' A new voice spoke. 'Good morning, Mrs Rippon. It's Miss Beacon here, of Critchlowe School.'

'Oh, I'm not Mrs Rippon. I'm her domestic help.'

'May I speak to Mrs Rippon, then, please?'

'I'm afraid not. She's in bed. Can I take any message?'

There was a pause. Then Miss Beacon said, 'Is Mrs Rippon ill?'

'Just a bit under the weather,' said Mrs Webb. 'She has these turns from time to time. I should try after lunch.'

'Are you alone with her?' inquired Miss Beacon. She sounded cautious. 'I mean, is there any other member of the family there?'

'Her daughter came last night. The older daughter, that is. Marjorie. But there's nobody here now. Bobbie's at school – but you'd know that, wouldn't you? Aren't I daft!' Mrs Webb gave a cracked laugh.

'Yes, of course. I just rang to ask how Mr Rippon is, but I won't disturb Mrs Rippon if she isn't well.'

'Oh, isn't that nice. Fancy you taking the trouble. I'll tell her when she wakes, if I haven't gone by then. I'm sure she'll be ever so pleased.'

'Thank you. Goodbye.'

'Bye-bye.' Mrs Webb replaced the receiver and made a face at the ceiling, above which her employer lay.

Fanny borrowed twopence from Mary Coppard just before afternoon school, went to the phone box outside the gate and dialled Bobbie's number. It rang for a long time and then Sylvia's voice answered.

'Hello.'

'Is Bobbie there, please? It's Fanny.'

''Course Bobbie's not here. Bobbie's at school. Isn't she? Aren't you at school?' She sounded blurred, as if she had just woken up.

'Yes, sort of. I just popped out. Sorry I bothered you. I expect I just got mixed up about Bobbie. She's probably in a classroom somewhere and I've missed her. It's such a big building, you know, and all rambly. I'd better be going now.'

'You wait a minute. Are you sure Bobbie's all right? What did you ring up for?'

'Oh, it's just me being silly. I'm awfully sorry.'

'Sorry, sorry – everybody's sorry! You know what Bobbie's father did, don't you? Drove his car into a lorry. I'm all alone here and everybody's sorry but that doesn't do me much good, does it? Where *is* Bobbie?'

Fanny did her best to imitate her father's professional voice. 'Bobbie will be home at the usual time, Mrs Rippon. It's quite all right. I just made a silly mistake. Goodbye.' She hung up and leaned against the side of the telephone box. What a mess! And how weird Bobbie's mother had sounded! But where *was* Bobbie? She glanced at her watch. She would just be in time for registration if she went now – and in any case, she could think of no immediate way to do anything useful. Very reluctantly, she left the phone box and went back to school.

Sylvia, still brooding about Fanny's phone call, lit a cigarette and poured herself another drink. The vodka and tonic had made her feel much better. There was quite a nice bit left in the bottle, too, so she would go on feeling better. In a minute she might get dressed and go downstairs. The house would be feeling better too, since Mrs Webb had been.

The telephone rang and Sylvia put her glass down carefully so as to have both hands free. She took the telephone on to her lap, lifted its receiver and said happily, 'Sylvia Rippon here.'

'Ah,' said the telephone crisply, 'good. This is Miss Beacon of Critchlowe School. I am sorry to have to tell you, Mrs Rippon, that Roberta left the school without permission this morning and has not returned. I telephoned you earlier but your home help said you were unwell.'

'I was,' said Sylvia. 'I still am.'

'I am sorry to hear that,' said Miss Beacon, 'and I am, of course, extremely sorry about your husband's accident. I must ask you, though, whether Roberta has returned home.'

'I already told that silly girl she isn't here,' said Sylvia irritably. 'And *she* said she'd made a mistake and she thought Bobbie was at school after all. Are you sure she's not there?'

'Perfectly sure,' said Miss Beacon. 'And I am beginning to feel that I may have to notify the police. As Headmistress of this school I am obviously bound to do everything in my power to discover the whereabouts of Roberta.'

Sylvia wished that she had left the telephone to ring. As if it was *her* fault that Bobbie wasn't there! 'I don't see what this has got to do with me, Miss Beacon,' she said. 'I got up this morning and saw my daughter off to school. Am I supposed to come with her and see that she stays there?'

'Your daughter,' said Miss Beacon icily, 'is a considerably disturbed child. I cannot tell what factors contribute to her disturbance but I can only say that your present attitude is not at all helpful, Mrs Rippon.'

Sylvia lost her temper. 'My God! You school teachers really have got a nerve, haven't you? If the kids pass their exams then it's all honour and glory to the school and the minute they do something wrong then it's the parents' fault. Look, if Bobbie's walked out of your school, Miss Beacon, then something went wrong at your school and it's your job to find her – and don't ring up trying to blame *me* for it!'

Miss Beacon's voice did not lose its rigid calm. 'I will assume that you are upset about your husband's accident, Mrs Rippon,' she said. 'And I will follow your suggestion that I find your daughter. I shall ring the police now.'

'You do that,' said Sylvia. 'You just do that.' The receiver clicked in her hand and she slammed it back on to its rest then reached for her glass. As she did so, the telephone lurched sideways on her lap and then pitched down on to the fluffy rug beside the bed. Its black rubber feet stared up at Sylvia reproachfully and its receiver, separated from its parent half, emitted an expectant dialling tone. 'You can shut up, too,' Sylvia said to it. She took a drink and refilled her glass. What a bloody awful business life was.

'I'd like a cheeseburger and chips, please,' said Bobbie. 'And a cup of coffee.'

'Got the afternoon off?' asked the boy behind the counter, eyeing her appraisingly. Bobbie blushed.

'No.'

'Just lunch break. Pity. Where d'you work, then?'

Bobbie was thrown into confusion by the necessity to lie and for a moment could think of no response. The boy was staring at her. 'In a shop,' she said desperately.

'Yeah? Which one? I'll pick you up, half past five.'

'No, you won't. I've got a date.' The thought of Colin had come to Bobbie's rescue.

'What – at half past five? He's keen, isn't he?'

'Yes, he is. He works in a shop, too, so we meet at half past five. And I don't want to go out with anyone else.'

'Oh, one of those *nice* birds,' said the boy ironically. 'OK. Here's your coffee. I'll bring your burger in a minute. And if you change your mind, you know where to come.'

Bobbie smiled at him, carried her coffee across to a table and sat down to think about Colin.

Bobbie left the Wimpy Bar at two o'clock, glancing at her watch and dashing out as though she was late for work. Otherwise she felt that the counter boy might strip off his apron and pursue her down the street. Almost to her disappointment, he gave no sign of even having seen her go.

She walked briskly along the street as a girl would who was on her way to work. If she walked at ten kilometres an hour, she calculated idly, she would have to cover over fifteen kilometres between now and half past four when Fanny would be home from school. Fifteen kilometres! And she had walked a long way already. This was the longest day she had ever known.

Perhaps she should go home. You never knew, her mother might be out. She could have gone to the hospital after all. She could have gone to the pub. What time did they close? Half past two? Yes, she might be in the pub. It would be much *easier* to go home.

Bobbie walked on for a while, then, rounding a corner, was confronted by a telephone box outside a post office. Fate, she thought. She went in, found twopence, and dialled her own number. A high pitched peep-peep told her that it was engaged. So her mother *was* in. That made things different. Bobbie retrieved her unused twopence and pushed open the stiff door. Now what? The school must have rung up to see if she was there. So her mother would know she had run away. Oh, how angry she would be!

Bobbie set off again. Her legs ached at the mere thought of walking fifteen kilometres. The new-found freedom of being away from school began to seem like a terrible form of imprisonment. She longed to talk to somebody and thought wistfully of Colin. She toyed with the idea of going to the bookshop where he worked; but Fanny's mother ran that shop. Bobbie knew exactly what *she* would say. 'Oh, goodness, Bobbie, I'm sure we can sort this out together. Hop into the car and you and I will go round and see Miss Beacon. She's not unreasonable, you know. She'll understand.' It was all right for Fanny's mother, thought Bobbie bitterly. People were always reasonable when she was about. But what about afterwards? Just look at the row Mary Coppard got into when her mother wrote a note saying she thought there was too much homework. It was weeks before Mrs Newley stopped making snide references to it. 'Now, *if* Mary's mother won't mind, perhaps you could bring yourselves to look at page fifty-three....' Oh, no. She couldn't risk the bookshop.

Suddenly she realised where she was. By a circuitous route, she had arrived back in Wilmot Road, not very far from the station. Hard on the heels of this recognition came an idea full of delicious promise. She would go and see if the man was still playing his trumpet in that funny building. What a *nice* thing to do!

But he wasn't. Bobbie stood outside the raw brick building almost weeping with disappointment. It had been such a small, innocent hope and now it was dead. The space it left was overwhelmingly empty.

As Bobbie turned to walk away, a girl of about twenty came out of the building, carrying a small child on her hip. She had almost waist-length dark hair, secured by an embroidered head band and she was dressed in a long skirt made from a printed cotton Indian bedspread. Over it she wore a man's shirt with the sleeves rolled up. Her feet were bare. The child, on the other hand, was dressed perfectly conventionally in a lemon yellow romper suit. It looked not more than a year old.

'Hi,' said the girl to Bobbie. 'Jesus loves you.' Her voice had the lazy warmth of California. The baby held out its pudgy hands to Bobbie and gurgled. Bobbie smiled. 'His name's Amos,' said the girl. 'And I'm Ruth. Hey, did you want to talk to someone here?'

'I – I wanted to hear the trumpet,' said Bobbie. 'I didn't mean to bother anyone. I just. . . .'

'You must come to our meetings,' said Ruth. 'Jeremiah plays 'most every night, as the Lord wishes. What's your name?'

'Bobbie.'

'Bobbie – are you on the dark side of the road just now?'

Because of the girl's American accent, the phrase did not strike Bobbie as being theatrical. It seemed, instead, to be a simple, true statement of how things were. Dark. Hard. That's how it was. Suddenly, she found that she was fighting back tears.

'Now, just you come on in,' said Ruth – and Bobbie, propelled through the door, found herself in a vast, sombre room almost the size of a village hall. The walls were adorned with Apocalyptic paintings of Biblical events and much of the floor space was covered with rows of wooden chairs but one end of the room had been cleared for use as a living area. Here, a crowd of girls and young men and children were clustered together on some old, battered arm-chairs which stood round a kitchen table covered with oilcloth. An immense kettle steamed gently on a gas stove and someone fingered a tune on a guitar. The young faces which glanced round seemed to Bobbie to be astonishingly beautiful, glowing in the dimness of the room. 'The Lord has sent us a new sister!' Ruth called to them, and instantly they responded with spontaneous excitement, jumping up and coming over to greet Bobbie. 'Praise the Lord!' they murmured, touching Bobbie with gentle hands and glancing up as though they addressed a familiar presence situated a little way above them. 'Praise Him.' 'Thank you, Lord. Amen.' 'Amen.'

Bobbie fought down a wild desire to giggle which was followed instantly by shame. They were absurd, these people, but so kind and so emotional that it was impossible to laugh. And they engendered a powerful family sense. They offered complete acceptance and comfort. They loved her. But why, oh, why? How could they? Overwhelmed, Bobbie burst into tears.

Gently, lovingly, she was led into a smaller room and sat down on a sofa with Ruth beside her. Ruth's baby perched equally happily on another girl's hip while handkerchiefs were proffered and a fair-haired boy with wire-rimmed spectacles brought Bobbie a cup of coffee, kneeling down at her feet to offer it in both hands, giving her his full attention. There was a weirdly formal, Biblical quality in everything they did or said and yet, somehow, Bobbie found this curious life-style familiar. Without consciously realising it, she found herself back in years-ago Sunday school, with oak-framed Jesus smiling gravely from the wall and wild flowers in jam jars. There is a green hill far away, without a city wall. Bobbie had come home.

'Dear Lord,' said Ruth conversationally, as if addressing a present but invisible member of the family, 'thank you for sending us this new sister to look after. Help us, Lord, to be wise in caring for her. We love you, Lord. Amen.'

'Amen,' they all chorused. They spoke the word again and

again, with a lingering enjoyment. And likewise, 'Amen,' said Bobbie.

Fanny rushed home from school and burst in through the kitchen door.

'Is Bobbie here?' she demanded.

Matthew looked up from the remnants of a tub of coleslaw which he was eating with his finger and shook his head.

'Are you sure?' persisted Fanny. 'Where's Dominic? Has he seen her?'

'Gone to get some glo-plug fuel,' said Matthew. 'Would you like some coleslaw? It's very nice.'

'No,' said Fanny. 'Look, I must find her. She ran away from school, you see.'

'Did she? Why?'

'I don't know why. That's just the point. I'd better try ringing up again.'

Fanny went into the hall and rang Bobbie's number. It was engaged. So Bobbie might be there. It could even be her on the phone, trying to ring Fanny. But then, it might be the police ringing her mother to say she had been found run over or something awful. No, it was no good sitting about waiting for news. Fanny had to find out, one way or another.

'I'm going round to Bobbie's house!' she called to Matthew. 'Be about an hour. I'll see to food when I get back.'

'There's something in the oven on pre-set,' Matthew shouted back.

'Great,' said Fanny. 'See you.' And she went out of the front door.

If only Bobbie lived a bit closer, she reflected, it would make things a lot easier. Perhaps it might be an idea to ask Stewart if she could have a bike. She'd never been keen on cycling and for the odd occasions when she really wanted one, she could borrow Matthew's. Dominic was too fussy about his. But then, there was the fiddly business of adjusting the saddle height – no, it was quicker to walk.

At last she arrived at Bobbie's house. She ran up the step-ping-stone path and rang the doorbell but there was no response. After a pause, she rang again. Oh, Bobbie, please answer. You must be there, she thought. Only twenty minutes ago the phone was engaged. *Somebody* is there, surely.

But nobody answered the door. Fanny turned away, sickened with disappointment. For the first time, she began to feel genuinely anxious about Bobbie. Until now, her disappearance had seemed exciting rather than alarming; an enviable bit of defiant skylarking. Now, it seemed more sinister. But people didn't simply *disappear*. Bobbie had to be *somewhere*.

Fanny began to retrace her steps, pondering deeply. Then she saw, hurrying towards her, Colin McIver, his jacket unbuttoned and his hair blown unkempt.

'Have you seen Bobbie?' he called as he approached.

'No. Have you?'

He drew level with her. 'No, I haven't. I came round here last night to see how things were with her father but I only saw her sister. Is there any more news from the hospital?'

Fanny shook her head. 'Not that I know of. But something else has happened. Bobbie ran away from school today. That's why I came to see if she's here, but I don't think she is. I rang the bell but nobody answered.'

Colin stared at the house, narrow-eyed. 'I wonder,' he said. 'I just wonder.'

He strode up to the front door and put his finger on the bell for a long time. From the pavement, Fanny heard it ringing faintly. But nobody came.

'You see?' she said. 'Honestly, Colin, I'm really worried about her.'

'So am I,' said Colin. 'With a mother like that, who wouldn't be? Hey – she wouldn't have gone to my house, would she? I told her, if she ever needed help, just to come.'

'M'm – I don't somehow think so,' said Fanny. 'Bobbie isn't practical, you know. She doesn't think of sensible things like that. She just sort of lives – in herself. You know what I mean?'

Colin shrugged helplessly. 'I've only met her once,' he said.

'So I don't know her all that well. But I hate to think of her having a bad time and I just wish there was something I could do about it.'

A police Panda car drew up beside them. The driver switched off the ignition, got out and went up the path to the Rippons' door where he in his turn rang the bell. He rang it several times, watched by Fanny and Colin, then came back down the path, looking up at the house. Fanny stared at him, worried. Why did the *police* want Bobbie?

'Excuse me,' she said cautiously, 'but do you know anything about Bobbie? I'm at the same school as she is. She's a special friend of mine.'

The policeman ran his eye over her uniform blazer and skirt, then turned to Colin. 'And who are you?' he asked. Colin bristled.

'I'm a friend, too,' he said. He was feeling slightly sensitive about unnecessary questions.

'This is Colin McIver.' Fanny introduced him. 'His sister is in Bobbie's class. But the funny thing is, when I rang up the phone was engaged. Somebody must be in.'

'We've had the same trouble,' said the policeman. 'Seems as if the phone is off the hook. We're getting the Post Office to put a howler on it. As to your friend, there's no news of her yet, I'm afraid, but I shouldn't worry too much. We get a lot of this sort of thing, youngsters going off in a temper and frightening everyone into fits in case they don't come back. Nine times out of ten they turn up the same day. Soon as they get hungry. Here, perhaps you'll know – did she have any money on her?'

'I don't think so,' said Fanny. 'She had her bus fare yesterday but she didn't say anything about any special money – but then, things had been so odd for the last couple of days, with her father's accident and everything. Bobbie's parents are a bit funny about money anyway. I mean, they've got plenty, but they don't give Bobbie any regular pocket money. They buy her things when she needs them and sometimes they'll suddenly give her a sort of present of some money, for no particular reason.'

'Never know where you are, do you?' said the policeman. 'Now, I give my nippers their pocket money Saturday mornings, regular.'

'But suppose she's been attacked?' burst out Colin, impatient with this casual chat. 'Or been run over or something?'

'Ah, now, that sort of thing we *do* know about,' said the policeman. 'If anything like that had happened, I wouldn't be standing here now, I can tell you that. No, I reckon your friend will turn up before dark. They nearly always do. Now, I'd best be on my way.'

He climbed into his car and drove off.

'I suppose he's right,' said Colin. 'It makes you hate them, the way they sound so casual about it, but they can't get worked up about every kid that plays truant. Anyway, I *hope* he's right.'

Fanny shook her head darkly. 'So do I,' she said. 'But I can't somehow believe it. Bobbie must have gone somewhere. Otherwise she'd have come to my house or gone home. I know she would.'

Colin grinned. 'The famous feminine intuition?'

'Yes,' said Fanny stoutly. 'Just that. And you can laugh as much as you like.'

Gordon arrived home to find a baby sitter drinking tea in front of the television set and Marjorie packing a suitcase.

'I've been trying to ring Mum all afternoon,' she announced, 'and the phone's engaged all the time. I think it's off the hook. Suppose she's had an accident or something? She isn't fit to be alone, Gordon, honestly – all the worry and....'

'All the booze, you mean,' said Gordon cheerfully. 'Your mum's all right, Marge. She just drinks too much. Don't we all?'

'Well, *I* don't,' said Marjorie crisply. 'And I must go and see if she's all right. You don't have to come if you don't want to, if you don't mind me having the car. Mrs Elkin says she'll stay the night, though, if we both want to go. I've packed for you.'

'Thank you,' said Gordon sarcastically.

Marjorie ignored him. 'Keron's had his bath and he's in his cot. I've made some ham sandwiches. We can't really stop for supper but if I drive, you can eat them in the car.'

Gordon sighed. 'The trouble with you is, you've got your head in a bucket of sand,' he said. 'You think that as long as things run nice and efficiently, everything can be taken care of. Don't you realise that there are some things that are basically and incurably messy? Your mother is one of them.'

'Gordon! What a beastly, untrue thing to say! Mum's had a difficult life, that's all. She's had to adjust to a lot of changes. She....'

Gordon held up his hand. 'Spare me the spiel,' he said. 'I know when I'm beaten. So we're all the victims of circumstance. A load of crap in my view, but I'm not going to argue. If I may change my shirt and say goodnight to my son, I'll join you in a minute.'

He started up the stairs and then paused and looked down over the banisters.

'All I can say is,' he added, 'those sandwiches had better be good.'

Mary Ross, singing happily as she ran into the bathroom for a quick splash before she went out to the Theatre Centre, was startled to find her landlady gazing pensively at the ceiling.

'Miss Ross, dear,' said Mrs Mallalieu gloomily, 'just look at that.' She thrust a piece of paper into Mary's hand.

'J. Dovedale, Builder,' read Mary, 'Estimate for....' She ran her eye down the items until she came to the last one. 'Bathroom, one hundred and eighty four pounds! That seems a lot.'

'Rather than pay such prices,' said Mrs Mallalieu, 'I shall go and live with my sister in Sheen. And what will become of my poor tenants, I do not know.'

And, retrieving the estimate from Mary's hand, she left the bathroom with dignity, sighing heavily as she went.

Sylvia woke to an unfamiliar sound – a kind of rough, high-pitched braying. She rolled on her side and waited for the noise to stop, but it went on and on. She flung out an arm in the direction of the alarm clock, which had obviously gone mad. She located its button and pressed it in, but the noise continued.

It seemed to be coming from the carpet. She wriggled to the edge of the bed and stared down. When her vision cleared, she saw the telephone lying upside down on the rug, its two halves widely separated. One of them, she was not sure which, was making the dreadful braying noise.

With some difficulty, Sylvia turned the telephone over and replaced its receiver. The noise stopped and she fell back, exhausted, on her pillow.

The telephone rang.

Sylvia groaned. She groped for the receiver and picked it up, more to stop the painful bursts of sound than through any desire for communication.

'May I speak to Mrs Rippon, please?' said a man's voice.

After a pause, Sylvia said, 'This is Mrs Rippon.' Her tongue felt too big for her mouth and the voice which she produced sounded remote.

'This is Sergeant Matthews, madam, of the local police. Your daughter was reported missing from her school earlier today and we have been trying to contact you.'

'Where is she?' asked Sylvia, confused.

'Well, I hoped you could tell me that, madam. Has she not returned home yet?'

'Returned – oh. I'm not sure. Jus' a minute.'

The receiver was saying something as she laid it on the bed, but Sylvia ignored it. She groped her way to the door, feeling very dizzy, and called, 'Bobbie? You there, Bobbie?'

The house was very quiet. Panic flooded through Sylvia's mind. She stumbled back to the telephone. 'She isn't here,' she said in anguish. 'There's nobody here. Where's she gone?'

'Thank you, madam,' said the policeman's voice immovably. 'I just thought she might have turned up. It would save us a job. And, madam, it would make things considerably easier if you will stay in contact. An officer came to your house this afternoon but could get no reply and the telephone. . . .'

'I was out,' said Sylvia. 'My husband's had an accident, you know. He's in hospital. I had to see him. I – oh, just a minute. Doorbell. May be her.'

The house reeled round Sylvia as she struggled down the stairs, grappled with the door and flung it open.

'Mum,' said Marjorie, 'are you all right? Gordon said he thought we'd better come.'

The Brethren were sitting round the big oilcloth-covered table eating stew out of white bowls. It seemed to consist mainly of carrots and potatoes but Bobbie though it tasted wonderfully good. 'I'd like to stay here always,' she said. 'It's so peaceful.'

'But you will stay,' said Ruth simply. 'The Lord sent you. It is His will. More stew?'

Bobbie laughed at the juxtaposition of religious and secular elements, then stopped herself guiltily.

'That's OK,' said Ruth. 'The Lord Jesus is among us and He understands our laughter as well as our tears. Laughter is good. He knows us.'

Gideon, the fair-haired boy who had brought Bobbie the coffee, nodded agreement.

'The Lord found me as well,' he said. 'I was on real hard stuff – in and out of one hospital or another – the drugs centre people said I was a hopeless case because I just didn't want to be cured. But I belong to the family now. They care for me and I care for them because the Lord is with us. We are in His hands.' His eyes shone with tranquil fervour behind their wire-rimmed spectacles.

'When I think back to life outside, it seems like a kind of hell,' said another boy. He was a tall, rawboned lad with big hands and feet whose dark hair and bushy beard left only the centre of his face visible. He had very intense, challenging blue eyes and Bobbie felt a little afraid of him. One of the girls laughed.

'Poor Jeremiah!' she said, 'you weren't appreciated, were you? Nobody would let you play your trumpet.'

Unruffled by her bantering tone, he said, 'It's a loud noise, a trumpet. You can't ignore it. My parents didn't mind so much when I was practising Purcell for the school orchestra but when I started playing jazz they kicked up no end of a fuss. I left school and went into digs but they didn't like it either and when I practised in my lunch hour at work I got the sack.'

'What did you work at?' asked Bobbie.

'I sold shoes.'

The Brethren burst into peals of laughter and when it died away Ruth said reprovingly, 'All people work for the Lord, each in his own way.'

'Praise Him,' agreed Jeremiah, 'but my way is through my music.' He spread his big hands in a shrug. 'If outside things interfere with the Lord's will, then you must discard them.'

The simplicity of his argument was too harsh for Bobbie. 'It's not always so easy,' she protested. Inwardly she felt a faint regret that the trumpeter was not, after all, a person she found specially attractive.

Jeremiah looked at her consideringly. 'Nobody said it was easy,' he pointed out. There was no rebuke in his tone but Bobbie blushed, feeling that she had said something absurdly naïve.

'I'm sure you'd like some more stew,' said Ruth tactfully, and doled another ladleful on to Bobbie's plate.

Bobbie ate some of her second helping of stew but found that her appetite had gone. 'I'll have to tell my mother,' she blurted out. 'Won't I?'

The stew she had eaten felt heavy in her stomach. She would have to go home. This was all a dream, a silly self-delusion. And yet it had seemed so safe, this gentle, unquestioning refuge. From inside here the life she had led until now seemed impossibly complicated and stressful. Out of utter weariness, she pushed her bowl away and buried her face in her hands.

'Do not fight the Lord's will,' said the fair-haired boy gently. 'Let him work in you.'

'Gideon is right,' agreed Ruth. 'Nothing is too difficult. Accept his plan for you.'

'But I *can't*!' cried Bobbie. 'It *isn't* simple! My mother will be frantic and my father's in hospital and Fanny will wonder whatever's happened to me – she's my friend, she's nice, but she'll be so worried – everyone will be worried! Don't you see, I must tell them where I am and then they'll come and take me way, I suppose – oh, I *wish* it was simple!'

'Of course your mother must know,' said Ruth calmly. 'Gideon, find me a piece of paper, in the name of the Lord.'

The Brethren, untroubled by Bobbie's distress, were going peacefully about their business, some clearing away dirty dishes from the table, some washing up in the kitchen and some playing with the half dozen or so children who seemed to belong equally to all of them. Others were bringing mugs of coffee which they placed before each recipient with the same grave attention which Bobbie had noticed before.

Gideon came back with pencil and paper and Bobbie, obeying Ruth's instructions, wrote down her name and address.

'Good,' said Ruth, handing the note to Gideon. 'And now, think in your soul, Bobbie, what does the Lord want you to do?'

Bobbie tried to think. 'I don't know,' she said helplessly. 'I'm just so tired. I don't know what to think.'

'Then it is the Lord's will that you must sleep,' said Ruth simply. 'No, don't argue. Come with me.' She pulled Bobbie to her feet and led her, protesting feebly, out of the room and up a bare brick staircase to the upper floor. There, she pushed open narrow swing doors which led into another enormous room which instantly reminded Bobbie of the hospital ward she had seen the day before, except that there were no screens or flowers or trolleys.

'Sit down,' said Ruth, pulling Bobbie down beside her on one of the little iron beds which stood in rows. 'Now listen. One of us will go to your house and tell your mother that you are safe. There is no need for you to worry. We will tell her where you are and say that you are sleeping.'

'But tomorrow—' began Bobbie.

'Tomorrow is still in the mind of God,' said Ruth. 'Jeremiah will be playing his trumpet at the Meeting tonight – you wanted to hear him, didn't you?'

Bobbie nodded. 'I'll just lie down for a bit,' she said.

'Good,' said Ruth. 'Now, dear Lord, watch over Bobbie and bring her your peace. Amen.'

'Amen,' echoed Bobbie. And, when Ruth had gone, she took off her skirt obediently, kicked off her shoes and lay down on the bed. She pulled the rough grey blanket over her, telling herself that she would only have a short nap – if, that is, she slept at all. And yet, as a drowsy warmth spread through her body, the prickliness of the blanket quite soon ceased to matter.

Fanny pushed open the green baize door into the auditorium, where a lot of the cast were already assembled.

'Hello, Fan!' said Ken Olliphant from across the piano. 'All perfect with the words, are we?'

'Not exactly *perfect*,' said Fanny. 'I learned a lot last night but things have been a bit chaotic today.'

'Ah, chaos, chaos,' murmured Ken, decorating his playing with a crossed-hands trill, 'the basic stuff of life.'

'My friend Bobbie ran away from school.'

'Did she now? Sensible girl. I feel like doing that ever morning. Here, talking of school, Fan, I've got one of your lovely Critchlowe ladies coming in this evening to grace us with her presence. I met her in some squalid hostelry, escorted by the dreaded Sparky Haynes.'

'Lee?'

'The same.'

'But who is it?' Fanny was astounded. One of the Critchlowe staff, in a pub with Lee Haynes? The mind boggled. Mrs Newley? Miss *Perkins*? The idea was hilarious.

'Some lissom thing rejoicing in the name of Mary Ross. It seems that she is bitten with the Muse, poor dear. Drama is, as they say, her Thing. I thought she could help to lick the choral speakers into shape. Make them sound a bit less like a duck-pond.'

Ken signed off his tune with a couple of chords and stood up.

'Right, me hearties,' he said to the cast generally. 'We'll do a bit of walk-through and see how it looks. Mark in the moves as we go. From the top, right?'

People started to move about, talking loudly and waving their scripts. Chaos again, reflected Fanny. Yes, chaos really was the raw material of the drama producer's art. She could see that. How wise Ken was, in his funny way! No wonder he hid his shrewdness behind that mask of light banter. He'd be a bit overpowering otherwise. Almost unbearably perceptive. Frightening.

Mary Ross slipped in through the door, unnoticed by Ken who was directing operations from the front row of the stalls. She caught Fanny's eye and smiled. Fanny smiled back politely. Miss Ross was wearing jeans and a long sweater and a lot of mascara. She looked very pretty. 'Where's Ken?' she whispered to Fanny.

'Sitting down. Front row, in the middle,' Fanny pointed to the back of Ken's head.

'Thanks,' said Mary, and made her way between the rows of seats to join him.

Fanny, watching Ken jump to his feet with unusual alacrity, seeing him smile at Mary, noticing his pleasure in looking at her, found herself shaken by miserable jealousy.

Fanny, walking home later from the Theatre Centre, felt acutely depressed. OK, OK, she could have gone round to the pub with the others. 'Grace us with your presence, Fan?' Ken had invited – but Miss Ross had been smiling beside him as if she was his bloody *wife*. And anyway, there was all that French homework to do for tomorrow, since the wretched school would not set it for more than one day ahead. She should have done it before she came out, but there had been all that business of going out to try and see Bobbie.

Oh, what a lot of things there were to think about, and none of them really in her power to act on effectively! Fanny allowed herself a brief daydream about her relationship with Ken supposing herself to be ten years older, then dismissed it angrily. It wasn't her fault that she'd been born so long after he was. But surely there was a possible communion of minds between people of vastly different ages? Nobody made a fuss when middle-aged women married men of about *seventy*. It was just another instance of unthinking convention.

Fanny's comfortless inner conscience gave her a sharp jab, reminding her that she herself was not above conformity when it suited her. This business of the French homework, for instance. Really, why did it have to be done for tomorrow morning? She could just say she had not done it. There would be an immense row; she might quite well be demoted to a lower division; eventually she might find that she was unable to take French as an O-level subject. So what, Fanny's argumentative half pursued. Did one have to accept the traditional blackmail?

Fanny sighed. It was the *crudity* of school which was so annoying, she thought. It was all based on the notion that a school was a kind of animated vegetable plot. You planted the eleven-year-old seedlings, fed them with facts, pruned them with discipline and watered them with competition then waited to harvest the crop. Oh, give me the jungle any time, Fanny said to herself, and stuff your old flower pots.

It was the sort of thing that made Bobbie laugh her scandalised, half-afraid laugh, Fanny thought. Irreverence always threw her into a panic of guilty amusement. Oh, Bobbie. Where could she be? Anxiety came flooding back. Surely no one could hurt Bobbie? She looked so small and vulnerable with her dark eyes and her crazy mop of frizzy hair. There was such a frail look about her pointed, always-white face. Only a maniac could hurt anyone who looked like that. But then, it was surely only maniacs who could hurt anyone?

Fanny reached her garden gate and paused for a moment, glancing up and down the road as if she half expected Bobbie to come running out of some gateway. 'Oh, Fanny, there you are! I've waited ever so long to see you!' But she was not there.

I'll ring up, Fanny thought. Right now. She must be home

by now but I'll just make sure. And then I'll get down to that blasted French.

Marjorie answered the telephone. 'Can I help you?'

'It's Colin McIver again – I rang Bobbie at six but she wasn't back and I just wondered if you've heard from her.'

'I'm very sorry, Mr McIver, but I'm afraid there's no news of her yet,' said Marjorie smoothly. 'If you'll give me your number I'll let you know if we hear anything.'

'How very kind of you.' Colin, feeling himself patronised, spoke with sarcasm but Marjorie ignored it.

'Not at all,' she said serenely, and replaced the receiver. As a dental nurse, querulous telephone calls were a part of her life.

Colin set out again along the empty streets in hopes of – of what? Of hearing Bobbie cry out from a parked car. Of finding her tied wrist and ankle on some building site. Of seeing her run headlong to him, her clothes torn and her face bloodstreaked. The McIver dream machine at it again, he mocked himself. That wee girl has gone to stay with some friends, you great fool. You've met her but once and yet you think she's your responsibility. Stupid. And yet if he just happened to be on the spot he might hear something or see something that could make all the difference. After all, the police couldn't be everywhere. It only *seemed* that they were.

Colin stiffened fractionally as a figure came into sight at the far end of the street, then relaxed again. It was too tall for Bobbie. As he drew nearer, he saw that the approaching person was a young man, despite the shoulder-length fair hair. He was walking purposefully and held a piece of paper in his hand which he glanced at occasionally. As always happens when two human beings meet in an otherwise empty landscape, a small tension began to exist between them and, as their paths crossed, they each felt the impulse to greet the other.

'Good evening,' murmured Colin and, 'God loves you,' said the boy called Gideon.

This is not the end of *The Doubting Kind*. In Part Two, called *All Who Love Us* ..., Bobbie and Fanny both have some dramatic events to cope with and, for Bobbie at least, the end when it comes, is a new beginning.